THE PERFECT RECIPE FOR MURDER

A Cloverleaf Cove Cozy Mystery

Annabel Allen

72218fin

AUTHOR'S NOTE

This is a work of fiction. Names, characters and situations are completely fictional and a work of the author's imagination. Any resemblance to any person, living or dead is purely coincidental.

Table of Contents

Prologue

They look just like pretty dollhouses all in a row.

That was what seven year old Arden Lynn thought the first and only time her parents took her to Cloverleaf Cove, a small coastal town off the coast of South Carolina, and that was thirty-three years ago. It was supposed to be a treat. One of those getaway vacations for the entire family. Her mom thought it would be fun to go somewhere quiet and serene in order to relax and renew before returning to the city and the daily grind of work. Her mother quickly learned, however, that quiet and serenity were foreign concepts to her two oldest children who spent the weekend making their displeasure known often and insistently.

It's too hot, too sunny, too boring, were often said with loud petulant whines that disturbed their mother enough to vow halfway through their vacation to never come back to the pretty sleepy little town nicknamed Coma Cove by Arden's older brother.

Unlike her siblings, little Arden never complained. She spent each day of their vacation on the beach staring—not toward the ocean, although that did take up a great part of her day—but at the magnificent houses on the ridge above the beach.

Beautiful, colorful houses with turrets and balconies befitting a princess.

She could never pick which one she liked the best, her favorite changing depending on where her imagination took her. She loved them all and she knew that someday, when she was grown, she was going to live in that sleepy little town in her very own dollhouse overlooking the ocean.

The memory of that vacation stayed with her for years, often drifting back whenever she thought about where she wanted to be in five years. That dreaded interview question popped up as she moved from job to job during her life.

Though she gave some job appropriate response, in her mind, the answer was always the same, Cloverleaf Cove, of course.

However, thirty-three years came and went as she drifted through life. She never found the time or the money to make it back to that little town on the coast and those little doll houses that captured her imagination so long ago.

Even if she had, her ex-husband would have made a permanent move impossible. A city boy at heart, he would never have been happy in a sleepy beach town. Kids and a white picket fence just wasn't his style, which he eventually admitted after years of promises of *someday* ...

Despite his admission, her dream never really died.

It was only a matter of time, she often thought to herself, and with her innate optimism and cheerful disposition, she was certain that her *someday* was just around the corner.

It wasn't until her husband ran off with his secretary, leaving behind a mountain of debt that she thought she would never get out from underneath, and that her certainty began to seriously waver. She had just started despairing of ever getting her dream home when something amazing happened.

It all started a few years before her divorce. One morning, she came upon an advertisement for a new business in town, called Mystery Games, Inc. The business was advertised as an intense mystery game, created by mystery lovers, for mystery lovers. It was billed as an international phenomenon with locations all over the world. According to the ad, players from all over the world traveled far and wide to pit their powers of deduction with others and for a small price, you could too.

To Arden, who had always loved mysteries of every shape and type, it sounded like great fun. To her husband, it sounded like a complete waste of time. She was about to toss the paper in the garbage when he suggested she go by herself. He had to work at home that weekend on some big project, he said, and she should go out and have some fun. Deciding he was right, she scraped together some money and went that very weekend, determined to win the game.

She lost. Came in dead last in fact. Missed every clue. Said the wrong things, but despite all that, she had the time of her life, so much so that she begged her husband to join her the next weekend. He agreed but to her disappointment, backed out at the last minute. Problems at work, he said before assuring her he would join her the next time.

She did a bit better that night in catching the clues and working things out, but she still didn't win. She remembered how her husband had laughed when she told him that she wanted to win. He thought it was impossible for her to win but still encouraged her to try again.

Practice makes perfect, he told her with a wry shake of his head. Determined to win and prove him wrong, she went back a few weeks later and tried their latest game. Once again, she went alone and once again, she lost, but by then she was hooked. She wanted to win, just once, she told herself. If she could do that, she'd quit as a happy woman. She went back as soon as she could and even repeated games she had already played in the hopes of figuring out what she had missed the first time. To her surprise, her husband continued to encourage her new hobby, going out of his way to find new opportunities for her to play while he toiled away late at night burning the midnight oil. It didn't take long for her to realize that he had an ulterior motive for getting her out of the house and it had nothing to do with work and everything to do with his new, young, pretty secretary.

Once the truth came out, Arden forgot the game for a while. It wasn't until some friends at work asked her to play with them that she had even thought about the game.

This time, unlike the previous times, something clicked. To her surprise, she won that night, and then again, and the weekend after that. As she racked up more wins, what began as a mere hobby soon turned into a full blown passion, as she eagerly sought out other Mystery Games, Inc. franchises near her home. It was only after she had won ten games in a row that she was given an invitation to play in one of the tournaments and the opportunity to earn some serious cash prizes, enough to get out of the debt her ex-husband left behind when he ran off with his girlfriend, and start building a sizable nest egg. Within a year, she had played twelve tournaments, racking up win after win and garnering some serious attention in their relatively small community of mystery players. So much so, that when the company announced that they would be sponsoring a tournament to beat all tournaments, Arden's name was one of the first names tossed out as a contestant.

When she received the official invitation, Arden jumped for joy. Not only would she have the chance to test her skills against the best players around the world, but also she had the chance to win a significant amount of money. Between the prize money and her savings, she'd have more than enough to live quite well in some far-off place in the middle of nowhere. Why she might even have enough to build her own business, she thought, as she prepared for the big day. So, with dreams of being her own boss firmly in her mind, Arden took a week off from work and made her way across the country to play.

The tournament was mostly a blur as she went through the motions of interviewing the suspects and putting all the pieces of the puzzle together. All she remembered clearly was the end when she was crowned the winner and handed a giant check by the president of the company.

Suddenly, after a lifetime of being poor, she had the freedom to go and do anything she wanted. She still remembered what she said when the president of the company asked what she was going to do with the money.

"I'm going home," she blurted out without thinking. *I'm finally going home.*

Within a month, she was standing in front of the Cloverleaf Cove real estate office with her new leather purse clutched in her hands, eagerly waiting for the real estate agent to arrive and open the doors.

Paige Graves, a friendly woman close to Arden's age with short black hair, dark brown eyes, and a bubbly personality quickly went to work asking all sorts of probing questions about the kind of house Arden was looking for.

A lifetime of practicality and frugalness dictated Arden's answers.

"I'm not entirely sure," Arden said with a careless shrug as though her future house wasn't something of monumental importance to her. "I guess I want a simple house. Nothing too fancy. I probably want at least two bedrooms, I suppose. Definitely one floor though. A little garden, maybe. Hopefully by the beach or at least within walking distance, and as near to downtown as I possibly can get."

Paige laughed as she reached for her purse. "Everything's near downtown. Just come with me. I have the perfect cottage for you."

And it was perfect, Arden thought as Paige walked her through the darling pink cottage about a half an hour later. It was just what Arden had asked for. Two bedrooms, a little garden, a mile from the beach and only a block from the center of downtown.

It was exactly what she asked for, but it wasn't for her, she thought as her gaze drifted to the colorful gingerbread houses on the ridge above town.

Arden pointed her finger towards the houses. "What about those? Are any of those for sale?"

Paige hesitated for a moment. "One but . . ."

Arden automatically turned to the door. "I'd like to see it, please."

Her heart began to beat faster as they drove up the winding road, flanked by palm trees towards an

6

unmanned guardhouse in the shape of a lighthouse. A pair of tall iron gates with a gold-plated cloverleaf in the center loomed in front of them. Paige waved a card in front of the card reader and the gold-plated cloverleaf in the center of the gates split open allowing them entrance. Arden had a brief sense of Deja vu as though she had driven through those gates once before but couldn't quite recall the experience. The feeling passed as Paige drove past one gingerbread house after another.

She had only seen the houses from afar as a little girl, but it was far more beautiful up close than she could have imagined. Two to three story Queen Anne style homes with turrets, balconies, wraparound porches and gingerbread trims stood behind perfectly manicured front lawns.

Arden felt like a little girl again as she looked from one side of the car, then back again as they passed each house. "It's at the end of this cul-de-sac," Paige said before finally making a right at a little park with colorful flowers, hedge bushes, wrought iron gates and old fashioned looking gas lamps.

"If you lived here you could use the garden for picnics or special events. There's a staircase from the garden which leads down to the beach," Paige said.

Arden's gaze immediately leapt to the charming two story, cotton candy pink Queen Anne sitting next to the garden. "It doesn't belong to that house?"

"No, it belongs to the community. In fact, all of the houses on this side of the lane have a walkway that runs along the back of their property line to the garden."

Arden was about to remark about how pretty everything looked when she noticed the house on the other side of the lane. Her mouth dropped open as she gaped at the gigantic five story tall gothic looking dark green Victorian mansion looming across from the garden and the much smaller pink house. "Wow," she said with wide eyed wonder.

"That belongs to a local celebrity," Paige said with a smile. "If you take the house at the end of the lane, I'm sure you'll meet her."

Keeping her eyes on the green mansion, Arden barely noticed the three story yellow house with pink trim standing next to it, nor the dark purple house that came into view next.

It was only when Paige turned her car around in the cul-de-sac that Arden tore her attention away from the green mansion enough to notice the other houses in more detail even spotting one she had missed during the drive. A dusty blue, almost silver Victorian with a large corner turret shaped like a lighthouse which sat next to the pink house and across from the yellow house. "Absolutely beautiful."

Paige was noncommittal as she turned off the car. Eventually, she took a deep breath and with a false note of cheer, brightly announced, "Well, we're here."

"Which one is for sale?" Arden asked breathlessly.

Paige cleared her throat. "The one behind us."

Arden turned her attention away from the other houses and turned around.

At the very end of the cul-de-sac sat a three story Queen Anne with a large wraparound porch and two turrets at each end. It was clear that years of neglect had taken a toll on the old mansion. Its once colorful trim had faded and chipped and the front yard was a depressing brown but that didn't stop Arden from breaking out into a smile at the sight of it.

Paige looked hopeful as she spread out her hands. "It's got great bones." Her voice was hesitant as she added, "It does need a bit of work but it's a lovely house."

Arden stepped out of the car and faced the mansion. Shielding her eyes from the sun's glare, Arden stared up at the front balcony taking in every detail. "It's beautiful."

A surprised smile broke across Paige's face as she pulled a set of keys out of her purse. "It is, isn't it? Come on, I'll show you the inside."

Nodding, Arden turned and glanced down the lane towards the other houses. "Absolutely beautiful."

Paige walked up the wide front steps towards the front door. "Watch your step," she warned as she pointed to a rotten board.

Arden tore her gaze away from the other houses and joined Paige on the front porch taking care to step around the damaged areas. She spotted bits of a muddy colored paint on the trim and asked, "What color did the gingerbread used to be?"

"Plum purple." Paige paused as she opened the door, her head tilted to the side. "Although I heard that, when it was originally built, it was a mixture of colors. I have pictures back at the office if you would like to see." She pushed open the double doors and stepped into a large foyer. "It's definitely a fixer upper, but I bet it would be gorgeous if someone took the time to take care of it."

Arden followed her inside the double doors to the right, not saying anything as Paige led her from a dusty parlor with giant bay windows to a large dining room with faded purple wallpaper and then finally to the galley kitchen.

"Obviously, this kitchen would need some work," Paige said. "The previous owners lived here since the 1960s and never bothered updating it, but there is a small bedroom back here. It used to be the servant's quarters a long time ago. I bet if you knocked down that wall behind the stove you could really open up this space."

Arden paid little attention to the kitchen, instead turning her attention to the backyard which was overgrown with weeds and partially dead bushes. A locked door leading to what looked like a sunroom caught her eye but before she could ask to see it, Paige opened a door near the stove and said, "It's got an unfinished cellar. The stairs are rather rickety and would need to be replaced but," she said quickly closing the door and pointing to a small hallway, "it has an attached garage. It was added in '79, I believe."

"Nice," she said turning from the sunroom.

"Are you a big reader?"

Arden nodded. "Very. I love reading."

"Oh, then you'll appreciate this," Paige said leading her into a hallway behind the kitchen. "You would have your very own home library." She stopped in front of a pair of French doors and flung them open, revealing a room with wooden paneling, purple shag carpeting and not a single bookshelf.

Arden arched an eyebrow. "This is a library?"

"The previous owners didn't care for reading but I've heard that shelves are behind the paneling," she said rapping her knuckles against the wood. She cringed as a panel fell forward and landed on the floor with a thud. Paige immediately directed her attention to the ceiling. "But just look at that chandelier. Isn't it gorgeous?"

Arden tipped her head back and admired the crystal chandelier. "Beautiful." Dropping her gaze from the chandelier, she turned in a circle and looked around. The room was larger than she expected a home library would be and much darker than any good library should be, she thought as she glanced through one of the windows noting that an overgrown box shrub was blocking most of the light from entering the room. Still, it definitely had promise.

"What do you think?" Paige asked hovering by the door.

Arden gestured to the door. "Did I see a sunroom off the kitchen?"

Paige's smile grew tight. "Yes, it . . . needs a lot of work. A tree fell through it during a storm we had last year. To be perfectly honest, it is a disaster." She lifted her eyebrows. "Would you like to see the rest of the house?"

Something about Paige's manner told Arden that the friendly real estate agent was used to being told no at this point in the tour so it came as quite the shock when she said, "Absolutely."

"Oh! Well, just follow me," Paige said with a bright grin as she led Arden to a large living room with another gorgeous fireplace and windows facing the front and side yards, then back into the foyer, up the staircase to the second floor and into a large corner bedroom at the back of the house. "There are five bedrooms including the one downstairs and one bath, but I bet one of those rooms could be turned into a master bathroom."

Arden glanced up at the plaster motif on the ceiling. "When was this house built?"

"1921."

"Are all of the houses around here that old?"

"Some of the wealthier members in town moved up here and built these houses in the nineteen twenties."

Arden ran her fingers over the brown and purple floral wallpaper. She peeked underneath a piece that was pulling from the wall to find an even uglier piece of wallpaper. "The other houses don't look like they were built in the sixties."

"Mod Victorian they called it. Our town founder, Gabriel Harcourt, owned most of this land. When he died, he left most of his land to the city to redevelop. He just had one condition. He insisted that any new buildings built here match the style of his mansion. You saw that giant green Victorian on the corner, didn't you? That was his house. His great granddaughter, Savannah, lives there now."

Turning in a circle in the middle of the room, her gaze roving from one corner to the next, Arden asked, "Are there any . . . historical restrictions?"

"To this one? No, these houses have gone through several renovations over the years. The last major one was in the seventies. If you are interested, you can do almost anything you like as long as you keep the general character of the house. I mean you couldn't bulldoze it and build a bungalow, for instance, but you can do almost anything you want to the interior." Turning her attention to the faded purple shag carpeting on the floor, Paige wrinkled her nose. "Obviously."

Arden paused in front of a pair of French doors and stepped out onto a large balcony which stretched from an enclosed bay window at one end of the house to an open turret at the other end. Hearing the roar of the waves against the shore, she glanced out toward the ocean and smiled. She could just imagine sitting out here every day enjoying her morning cup of tea and admiring God's creation. She glanced up with a smile at the sea gulls flying overhead, then down towards the ships sailing in the distance. Her smile fell as her attention dropped to the backyard and its hip high weeds.

Turning away from the backyard, Arden walked along the balcony towards the open turret, then around the side of the house to another open turret located at the front of the house. She glanced at the blue house next to her and then made her way back to the other turret.

A white wicker table and chairs would be perfect here, she thought, already mentally shopping in her head. She ran her hand along the balcony, mentally picking out the paint colors she wanted for the gingerbread trim. Feeling something rough under her hands, she glanced down at the railing where someone had scratched the initials GK into the wood.

"Look at that view," Paige said joining her on the balcony, "I never get tired of it."

Arden smiled. "You come up here often?"

Leaning out over the railing as far as she could, Paige pointed to a pink turret just visible over the top of the blue house. "That one's mine."

"You own the pink house?" At Paige's nod, she asked, "How long have you lived here?"

"Three years." She looked hopeful. "If you buy this place we'd be neighbors."

Arden unconsciously traced the initials in the railing with her finger. "Do you like it here?"

"Love it. I couldn't imagine living anywhere else and this is coming from a girl that never thought she'd leave Nashville."

"What brought you here?"

Paige tucked a lock of her hair behind her ear. "My father-in-law owns the local funeral home. He got sick one year and so we came to help take care of him. It was only supposed to be a temporary visit but my husband and daughter didn't want to leave, so we stayed. Patrick works at the hospital a few miles from here and our daughter, Kelly, is in college. She just finished her freshman year and she is here for summer vacation. She's studying to be a doctor just like her father," she said with obvious pride in her voice. "As soon as she's finished studying, she says she's moving back here." A frown tugged at her lips. "That'll be years from now though."

"I'm sure the time will fly by."

"I'm not so sure." There was a pause. "It takes years to become a doctor. First, there's undergrad, then there's med school, and then residencies. I just keep thinking it was only a few years ago that she was right here by my side. I mean she's here now but she spends so much time on her phone, I barely see her." She sighed. "It's kind of boring around here now that she's all grown up." Her eyes widened in surprise at her own admission. "I mean, it's quiet here. Peaceful." She gave Arden a wry grin. "I really do love it here. It's just now with Kelly gone most of the year and Patrick at the hospital all day, it's a bit lonely."

"You have your own business, so that must keep you busy," Arden said trying to cheer her up.

"I only work part time," Paige said with a dismissive wave of her hand. "There's just not enough business to keep me occupied during the day."

Arden studied the woman out the corner of her eye. "How long has this house been on the market?"

A little sigh escaped Paige's lips. "Five years. I've been trying to sell it ever since I arrived. You're the first person in over a year I've gotten to come upstairs."

After Paige's confession, Arden felt a bond starting to form between them. She leaned a hip against the railing and turned toward the other woman. "Okay, what's wrong with it?"

Paige seemed surprised by the question. She jerked a thumb towards the house. "Did you get a good look at that kitchen?" She wrinkled her nose again. "And that purple shag carpeting? And why would anyone board up bookcases? Honestly, what were they thinking?" She turned her disgust towards the backyard. "And just look at that. I swear, there's no telling what's under all that mess."

Arden shook her head. "Unless there's some sort of foundational or structural problems, there doesn't seem to be anything that can't be fixed."

"Oh, there's not. The sunroom needs the most work of course. The porch and the roof needs to be patched up too, but it's not too bad considering how long it's been neglected. It just needs a little attention."

"Then why has it been on the market for so long?"

Paige grimaced. "The former owners call this their show place. Let's just say the price is a bit *high* for a fixer upper."

"How high?" She whistled after Paige told her how much the owners were asking for it.

"Each year that the house deteriorates, Mr. Oakley tacks on another couple of thousand dollars to the asking price. He pays me to keep the front yard mowed and make sure no one breaks in, but he doesn't seem to be concerned that I can't seem to sell it. He just keeps saying that if someone wants it bad enough they'll pay what he's asking for it."

Arden looped an arm around the turret's beam and looked out towards the ocean. For once in her life, she had the money to buy what she wanted and what she wanted was this house. Nodding to herself, she said, "Tell Mr. Oakley he's right."

Chapter 1

Mr. Oakley, happily, if not a bit smugly, Paige informed her, accepted her offer the very next day. The house inspection took a little longer than expected but everything worked out in the end.

As Paige said when she first showed her the house, *it has good bones* and she was right.

Later, as Arden replayed the moment in her mind, she laughed at the quaint expression but she had to agree. The house was beautiful inside and out. All it needed was some tender loving care.

No sooner had the ink dried on the contract than Arden contacted a contractor in town and set them to work on her dream house. The next four months flew by as she traveled back and forth from New York to Cloverleaf tying up loose ends during the week and working with her contractor and interior designer during the weekend.

It was funny thinking of her old life as a loose end, but that was what it was. Out with the old and in with the new was her favorite phrase as she started preparing for the move.

A nice quiet life was what she wanted. One where she could spend her days lying on the beach and her nights in her library reading. Part of her fantasized about starting a new romance. Hopefully, it would be one that was better than the last one, and that wouldn't leave her brokenhearted and in debt. Whenever those thoughts about her old life intruded, she quickly shoved them aside and focused on the future. Her new life was in Cloverleaf now. Things would be different here.

It was odd how during those last four months in New York, she started feeling like a visitor in what was still her home. Instead of the daily grind of working all day, sitting on the subway for over an hour before grabbing a quick bite to eat then collapsing in front of the TV, she spent her days looking at paint samples and color swatches or running from one furniture store to another, selecting the perfect pieces to go into her new house.

When she wasn't doing either of those things, she was at the gym getting her body back in shape after years of neglect. Now that she didn't have to spend her time working and commuting back and forth, or playing the mystery game she had once been so fond of, she found she had much more time to spend on herself. It was a good feeling coming home at the end of the day, refreshed and energized instead of mentally exhausted and bone weary.

While she worked on getting healthy, her contractor worked on the house, starting with the kitchen.

"Has to go," she insisted when she first walked through the house with him at her side. He readily agreed, coming up with a new layout for the back end of the house. Out with the Formica and in with the marble. The small bedroom at the back was removed and it became part of a larger kitchen. The narrow sunroom was completely demolished and in its place, a newer sunroom was added. One that extended out from the kitchen in the shape of an octagon and was large enough for her new kitchen table and chairs.

The dining room at the back of the house next to the kitchen was converted into an open living room and the former living room at the front was converted into a formal dining room. The parlor was kept the same, needing only a coat of paint on the walls and varnish on the hardwood floors to make them sparkle.

She chose floral patterns with pastel colors and antique white wainscoting and cabinetry for every room, insisting that her house be as light and airy as possible. The only darkness came from the hardwood floors and some of the wooden furnishings which ended up in the library.

She spent the most time designing the library. The shag carpet and wood paneling in the library was removed, and underneath to Arden's delight, the workers uncovered built in shelves and hardwood floors.

She added a desk where she could work on whatever project captured her fancy and large comfy chairs by the windows for reading. Her favorite part of those four months was the days she spent at bookstores scouring the aisles for books to add to her shelves. She couldn't wait to see them in her library just waiting for her to sit down and read.

Upstairs, she took the two bedrooms at the back of the house as her master bedroom, converting the one with the turret into a luxurious master bathroom and walk-in closet for her new wardrobe.

The third floor was just attic space, which she left alone, only adding paint to the walls.

When she left her old life, she left it all behind except for some sentimental trinkets which would fit in a shoebox. Everything else she gave away to family or Goodwill. She wasn't sure what she was going to do with the attic or with the basement, but she figured that could wait.

She had all the time in the world to figure out what to do with those spaces, which was a good thing, she thought as she stepped into her new kitchen. She was going to need projects to keep her busy.

She opened a box, placed it on the island and pulled out her new copper pots and pans. As often as she dreamed of a life of leisure while working eight to five, she knew that she'd eventually get bored, so she had set aside things to keep her occupied. Cooking was one project she had assigned for herself, buying as many cookbooks and the best pots and pans she could get her hands on. She wasn't sure what she was going to do with them yet—her idea of cooking being a take out dinner or reading the instructions on the back of a box—but she was going to learn.

A wasp flew past the kitchen window just then causing her to frown at the jungle that was her backyard. What a mess, she thought as she looked at the overgrown jungle of bushes, grass and trees.

While she was in New York, Arden let Paige hire a landscaper for the front and side yards. Arden had insisted the backyard be left as was. Paige looked at her as if she was crazy when she told her that she didn't want it touched, but she did as Arden requested. As far as Arden was concerned, the backyard was something special and she wanted to be personally involved in its design. Another one of her future projects to keep her busy, she had decided.

The only problem was that she knew about as much about gardening as she did about cooking, and now that she was face to face with the jungle, she wondered if she might have made a mistake.

Setting aside the pots and pans, she reached inside a box lying next to the French doors and pulled out a wind chime. She smiled at the pretty sound it made as she carried the chimes out to a large pink crepe myrtle near her back door. It wasn't much, but it would have to do until she figured out what she was going to do, she thought as she hung the chime on the lowest branch she could reach.

Another wasp drew her attention upward towards a giant nest above her head. She inwardly cringed as one came far too close for comfort. She stepped off the patio and onto a stone paver. Feeling something crawling on her, she slapped at her leg, only to realize it was just grass brushing up against her calf.

She was going to have to bring someone in to mow at least, she decided suddenly. She could probably do it herself, but having lived in the city her entire life, mowing wasn't exactly something she was used to doing and if she were going to do it, she'd rather not start with the jungle. Once the grass was cut, she could reassess what needed to be done. Not all of it was a mess after all.

Tall, perfectly manicured hedges separated her property from her neighbors on either side of her. Her side of the hedges were a bit overgrown and there were a few bare patches and a rather large gap where an old shed had once stood, but other than that, it seemed in pretty good shape

At the very back of her property was a slightly shorter hedge, which separated her backyard from the brick walkway that ran along the back of the houses. Arden would have preferred it if it was much shorter than it was. The way the yard sloped down, all she would need was to cut another foot or two off and she would be able to see the ocean from her back patio.

What might be a bit more difficult to fix was the gate and the two pillars flanking it in the center of the hedge. One of the lanterns that used to sit on top of the pillars was lying on its side next to the hedge. Fixing that was going to require outside help. She also needed to find a pair of bolt cutters in order to remove the chain and padlock keeping the gate closed.

She was going to need help removing the dead tree near the gate too. Luckily, it wasn't a tall tree, but it was still going to take some effort to remove it.

The only other problem that she could see was on the other side of the sunroom. The backyard had once been enclosed on either side of the house by hedges as well, but several years ago, the previous owners had removed the hedge to make room for an extra carport that never had been completed. Now, all that was left was an unsightly muddy entrance to the backyard.

She was contemplating adding a gate similar to the one in the back when she noticed the tall grass and weeds in front of her swaying in an unusual pattern.

Must just be the wind, she thought idly for a moment before frowning in concern. Something about the pattern of the movement caught her eye as being unnatural.

Her frown deepening, she shielded her eyes and stepped forward to get a better look at whatever it was causing the grass to move in such a way. The sound of dead dried leaves crackling caught her attention and she took a hesitant step back towards her home.

Her first thought was of snakes. Of course, there were snakes, she thought with a shudder. Her backyard was probably a snake heaven.

Heart pounding, she took another step back. She was wondering how quickly she could get her landscaper to come back when whatever was under the grass suddenly stopped.

She paused, staring at the grass warily.

Suddenly, whatever it was took off again, coming straight for her.

Surprise caused her to scream and jump back. The moment she did, her foot collided with a loose brick in the patio and she fell back just as a brown ball of fur burst out of the grass and ran towards her barking madly.

Arden, flat on her back, watched in relieved amusement as a rambunctious puppy began running circles around and sometimes on top of her.

She didn't know much about dogs, not having had any of her own, but she could at least recognize a cocker spaniel when she saw one.

She rose onto her elbows and held out her hand for the pup to sniff. Once the necessary greeting was completed, she ran her fingers over his golden head. "Well, hello there."

Just then the sound of a man calling out, "Lucky" at the top of his lungs caught her attention. She caught the puppy by his collar and said, "I think your master's calling you, little one." The puppy barked his displeasure at having been caught and began twisting and turning in an attempt to get away.

Just then, a handsome man perhaps around her age, judging by the touch of silver in his blond hair, slipped through the small gap in the hedge to her right. Spotting her on the ground, he quickly rushed across the yard towards her.

Kneeling next to her with an apologetic look on his face, he said, "I'm so sorry. What did he do?"

As soon as she saw his concerned blue eyes, staring down at her she was at loss for words. The only thing she could think was that he was quite possibly the handsomest man she had seen in a long time.

His eyes became more concerned as she continued to gape at him. "Are you all right?"

Arden suddenly became aware at how she must look and laughed to cover her embarrassment. "Yes, of course."

"I'm so sorry, I don't know how he got out of the yard," the man said as he helped her to her feet. He towered over her, his strong hand, lightly holding her elbow.

She reached up a hand, pushing her dark brown hair back off her face, her eyes widening when she discovered a leaf in her hair. His words became background noise as she quickly checked her appearance.

Why had she chosen to wear an old t-shirt and shorts of all things? True, she was moving in but it wasn't like she was the one carrying the boxes off the truck.

"I've been meaning to take him to obedience class…"

She dusted some dirt off her leg. "Mmmhmm."

"…he's only a few months old…"

Suddenly, he smiled and she felt weak in the knees. Good grief, get hold of yourself, Arden scolded herself as he looked at her strangely. You act as if he's the first handsome man you've ever seen.

"…I've only had him for a month but he's got a lot of energy…"

She managed a note of agreement as she straightened her t-shirt. Her fingers came across something wet and grimy and she finally tore her attention away from his eyes to stare at the muddy wet mess on her blue t-shirt.

She glanced back up as he muttered a curse. "Sorry," he said automatically almost distractedly as he looked around. "Did you see which way Lucky went?"

The sound of barking and a man's gravelly voice shouting, "Get out of here, mutt!" caught their attention.

Suddenly, her handsome new neighbor was off like a shot, calling Lucky's name. He managed another apology before dashing around the sunroom towards the hole in her hedge and disappearing from view.

Arden glanced down and cringed at the dirt that marred her white shorts. She glanced behind her noticing even more dirt on her rear end. She tried brushing it off but that just seemed to make it worse.

"Hey, Girlie!"

Arden's eyebrows rose up her forehead at the sound of a masculine raspy voice whispering to her from the hedges to her left. Girlie? It had been years since anyone had called her a girl. She glanced over at the hedge, more amused than offended.

"Hey, come here," he ordered when she didn't move fast enough to his summons.

She peered through a bare patch in the hedge. An elderly man with a full head of bushy white hair stared back at her.

"What did you scream for?" he whispered in a low gruff tone.

"Well, I—"

"Lower your voice." He glanced over his shoulder before dropping his voice even lower. "Did you find her?"

"Who?"

"What do you mean who? Did you find *her*? Did you find Ivy?"

"I don't have any idea who Ivy is and no I didn't."

He peered closely at her face, studying it. After a moment, he pulled back with a sigh, the tension in his shoulders clearly dissipating. "No, I guess you didn't." His upper lip lifted in a cruel smile. "If you had, you'd still be screaming."

Chapter 2

Arden's eyes widened. "I beg your pardon."

"What were you screaming for?" the man asked once again in annoyance.

"The puppy scared me."

A look of disbelief came over his face. "The puppy…?"

"What did you mean by I'd still be screaming if I found Ivy? Who is Ivy?"

"No one. Mind your own business," he said over his shoulder, leaning heavily on his cane, "you'll live longer."

"Hang on a second," she said as a feeling of unease washed over her.

"Look, here, just never you mind." He glanced over his shoulder again before muttering in disgust, "Humph, the puppy scared her."

He's crazy, she thought as he painfully ambled away. Absolutely nuts.

She shook her head in bemusement as she walked away from the hedge and back into her house. One look at her reflection though wiped the smile off her mouth. "So much for making a good impression on the neighbors."

She tore another leaf from her hair before marching upstairs to the master bedroom.

Forty-five minutes later, she returned to unpacking her new cookware.

"Wow!"

Arden glanced up surprised to find Paige standing behind her with a look of amazement on her face.

She laughed at her friend's expression. "Why do you look so amazed? You've been in here a dozen times in the last few months." Paige had been a Godsend, pitching in to help, sending her pictures back and forth and keeping her informed as to what was going on while Arden was in New York. In that time, she had become a dear friend to Arden. She often felt guilty for relying on her so much but then Paige would say, "What are neighbors for" and before Arden knew it, whatever she needed was done.

"I'm not talking about the house," Paige said. "I'm amazed at you. The day I moved in, I wore an old sweatshirt and sweatpants. Nice heels by the way."

Arden cleared her throat as she glanced down at her red high heels. "Yes, well I didn't want to shock the neighbors so thought I should dress up. Where have you been?"

"At the pink cottage I showed you when you came here. I'm having an open house. I don't know why I can't sell that house. It's absolutely darling." Paige turned in a circle as she surveyed the kitchen and the living room before walking over to the newly restored sunroom. "Love the furniture. It looks like a completely different house. Oh, by the way, sorry for barging in but," she said jerking her thumb over her shoulder, "did you know your front door's wide open?"

"It is? I must not have closed it all the way when the movers left today." Arden blinked in surprise at her own statement. She couldn't remember a time when she wasn't always checking the door locks and windows, making sure everything was locked down tight as a drum.

A slow smile crossed her face as she set the empty box aside. What a difference a change in location made. It was so nice not to have to worry about such things. "And you know you don't need to apologize. You're always welcome here."

"Well, I just came to warn you, you've got an audience."

"Oh?" Arden lifted her head and looked over the island towards the windows on either side of the front door. A group of people was standing on the other side of the street milling around staring at her house. "Who are they?"

"Your new neighbors. They're all itching to get a look inside. I told them they're just going to have to wait."

Speaking of neighbors, Arden thought as she stared pensively out the window towards the purple house. "Do you know who Ivy is?"

"Ivy who?"

"I don't know. One of our neighbors was looking for her."

The doorbell rang.

Paige adjusted the bangle bracelet on her wrist. "I guess now would be a good time to tell you that there's some things I didn't tell you about our neighbors."

Arden looked at her friend in amusement. "Such as?"

A woman's rich southern voice called out from the hallway. "Hello?"

"Some of them are really pushy," Paige whispered in a sotto voice as a stunning older woman with white blonde hair and an authoritative manner strolled in.

"I heard that," the woman said with an amused look.

29

Immediately, Arden was struck by a sense of recognition as snippets of old television shows floated through her mind, all of them featuring the same blonde haired blue-eyed girl. Arden's mouth slowly fell open in surprise at finding one of her childhood heroes standing in front of her.

Paige smiled as she waved a hand between Arden and the woman. "Arden, this is Savannah Mae Addams-Winchester. Savannah used to be on TV." Her brow furrowed. "What was your show's name again? Sutton and Gross?"

"Sutton and Grimes," Arden automatically answered for the former actress. "Oh, my gosh. I'm a huge fan of yours. I think I saw every episode of *Sutton and Grimes* at least three or four times and that haunted house movie you did still gives me the shivers. You were like my favorite show when I was a teenager." Realizing she was still shaking Savannah's hand, she forced herself to let go of the woman's hand. "You were amazing."

Savannah smiled sweetly as she gently rubbed her fingers. "Well, how sweet of you to say. Thank you."

"Whatever happened to your co-star? The one who played Grimes. I used to have the biggest crush on him."

"He works at his father's car dealership in Vegas now," Savannah said with a sad sigh, tucking her trademark long blonde curly hair behind her ears. "Anyway, I'm just so glad you're finally here. Paige has talked about you so much that I feel like I know you. I can't begin to tell you how many times your name has come up at the Jolly Green Giant."

Arden blinked. "The what?"

Savannah glanced past Arden's shoulder to the backyard. "That's the name of my house, dear."

"Savannah and I came up with names for all the houses on this block," Paige said. "Mine is the Pink Flamingo, all because I once put a pink iron flamingo in my yard."

"Oh, I see," Arden said, "and what is mine?"

Paige's eyes twinkled. "The Gray Ghost."

Arden laughed. "I have a ghost."

Savannah waved a dismissive hand. "Oh no. This house was just so bleak and dreary looking for the longest time that it was the first thing we thought of. We used to say it was haunting us. Here but not here, if you know what I mean. Houses just aren't themselves without someone living in them." Her gaze fell once more to the garden. "We must come up with a new one. Something more fitting."

Just then, the sound of loud angry voices caught their attention. Curious, one by one they filed out of the room, down the hallway and into the foyer. They stepped out onto the porch and looked across the street.

Two men, one middle aged and extremely tall with rugged good looks, a heavy muscular build and a penchant for cowboy boots, the other older and stooped with thinning white hair and a cane stood on the side walk, their angry voices carrying as they got into each other's faces.

Arden recognized the middle-aged man right away. His name was Duncan Thorpe and according to Paige, he was the best landscaper in town and by far the most reasonable. While Arden was in Chicago, Paige had hired him on her behalf to do the front and side yard. Based on how her lawn turned out, she had to agree with Paige's assessment. The other man, while she didn't know his name, was the same man who had yelled at her from behind the hedge an hour ago.

Savannah sighed. "Looks like Tweety Bird and Barney are at it again."

The older man angrily gestured with his cane towards a red sports car parked in the yellow house's driveway. Duncan pursed his lips together as he vehemently shook his head.

Arden inclined her head. "I take it Tweety Bird belongs to the yellow house?"

"That's right."

"And Barney?" she asked.

"The purple one."

Arden hid a smile. "Of course. Which one is which?"

"Tweety Bird is owned by Duncan Thorpe," Paige answered.

"Who is the other one?"

"Bruce McCallum," Savannah said then with a distracted note in her voice added, "Retired salesman, I believe. Don't really remember what he sold. Doesn't matter. If you're curious, I'm sure he'll tell you. Stay away from him if you can."

"Why?"

Savannah casually leaned against the doorjamb. "He's as mean as a snake. I feel sorry for his granddaughter, Wendy, trapped in that home with him day in and day out."

They turned their attention back to the men outside, as their voices grew even more strident.

"What are they fighting about?" Arden asked.

"Who knows," Paige said, annoyance coloring her voice. "Last time it was over a tree branch that fell on Bruce's property."

Savannah wrinkled her nose. "Bruce is mad because he thinks that Duncan has been paying too much attention to his granddaughter, Wendy." She glanced back at Arden. "He's worried that, if those two get together, Wendy's going to put him in a home. He complains about everything that Duncan does. Last week, he called the cops on him."

"What for?" Arden asked.

"Trespassing," Savannah responded. "He accidentally stepped on Bruce's yard and crushed a daisy."

"Duncan doesn't help things," Paige said. "He's constantly doing things to upset the old guy."

They glanced back to the two men whose voices were growing more strident by the second.

Arden glanced at the car, only then noticing the red bow on the hood. "Who's the car for?"

"Probably for Julie, Duncan's niece," Savannah said. "He's been taking care of her ever since her mother abandoned her fifteen years ago. He absolutely dotes on that girl." She clamped her hand on Paige's arm. "You should have seen the diamond necklace she was wearing the other day. It was absolutely gorgeous."

Bruce, his face red, lifted his cane over his head. He started to raise his arm back when the handsome next door neighbor Arden had met earlier intercepted him. She watched as he quickly stepped between the two men, easily pushing them apart.

Savannah sighed in annoyance. "It was just starting to get interesting before the Silver Fox stepped in."

"The Silver Fox?" Arden repeated quickly.

"His name's Max Ferris," Paige said, "and he's renting the blue house next door."

"With his wife?" Arden asked idly as she traced the pearls at her neck with her fingers.

Paige exchanged a look with Savannah before wrapping an arm around Arden's shoulders. "Actually," she said leading Arden away from the door, "he's single."

"And the very reason why I stopped over," Savannah added.

Arden glanced over her shoulder at the former actress. "You came over to tell me my next door neighbor is single?"

"No, I came to invite you to a party tomorrow night. The first Thursday of every month, we all get together at one of our homes for a little neighborhood party. I'm hosting this month and would like you to come join us."

"Oh, that sounds lovely. Thank you. Is there anything I can bring?"

"No, just yourself," Savannah said. "We want to introduce you and Max to the neighborhood. He's new here too."

Paige raised an eyebrow. "He's been here for three months, but we've yet to get him to come to the party. What makes you think you'll be able to get him to come this time?"

"Because he promised and I think he's a man of his word." Savannah tapped Paige's arm. "Since he's outside, why don't you remind him about the party? I think he's been avoiding me."

Paige sighed as she stepped out onto the porch. "I'll try but don't hold your breath."

"I take it he's not the sociable type?" Arden asked.

Savannah's pursed her lips together. "Bruce put him off. Told him a bunch of nonsense about how everyone must bring a dessert and be prepared to discuss the latest book assigned."

"There's a book?"

"Occasionally."

"And dessert?"

"Oh, most definitely," Savannah added with a grin. "We have a bake-off competition every month. Everyone brings a homemade dessert and we award a prize to the winner but you're not required to bring anything. It's just for fun." Savannah stepped out on the porch. "All you have to do is show up and be ready to meet your neighbors." She held up a cautioning finger. "But if you do want to bake something, I must insist that it be home made. Whatever you do, do not go to the bakery in town."

Arden's eyebrows rose in surprise. "Oh, okay. It sounds wonderful. How many people do you expect to be there?"

"Probably no more than ten. It's usually a very small gathering." Savannah lightly jogged down the steps. "Seven o'clock at the Jolly Green Giant. Don't forget."

"I'll be there." Arden waved goodbye as Savannah turned and made her way down the porch. She smiled as she looked out at her new neighborhood. For the first time, she truly felt at home.

Everything was finally falling into place. Now all she had to do was come up with some dessert to impress everyone. There was no way she was going to go empty handed. Her mother raised her better than that.

A squeal of excitement caught her attention and she glanced out her door. A young woman with dark hair and a big grin had her arms around Duncan Thorpe. She turned and clapped her hands while jumping in place as

Duncan dangled keys from his hand. Snatching the keys out of his hand, she stood up on her tiptoes and kissed his cheek before dashing to the new car. Must be Duncan's niece, Julie, Arden thought while watching the girl. Arden found herself smiling as the excited girl jumped behind the wheel and revved the motor.

Bruce McCallum didn't seem to share her enjoyment at the heartwarming scene. Snarling, he shook his head before collecting his mail out of the mailbox then turning and walking back to his house. He angrily stomped up his steps, the tip of his cane striking the wood with a loud thump.

His angry voice floated through the air as he pounded his way to the front door. He took one look outside again before slamming the door shut with a resounding thud.

Maybe I don't want to get to know every neighbor, Arden thought as she closed her door.

She started to step away, but for some reason she couldn't explain, she stopped and locked the door behind her.

Chapter 3

Arden awoke the next day happier than she had ever been before. With nowhere to go and nothing pressing to do, she snuggled into her blanket determined to get a few more minutes of sleep. However, every so often, her eyes would pop open and she'd look at her pretty bedroom with its soft crème colored walls and white lace curtains before lightly dozing off again.

The slamming of a car door outside finally woke her up fully and she glanced at the clock on her nightstand. She sat up in surprise to find it was nearly ten o'clock. Unused to whiling away a morning in bed she kicked off her bed covers and slid out of bed.

Ten minutes later, she padded out on her balcony with a cup of coffee in her hands. Her builder had been the one who suggested adding a coffee station in a small nook between the bathroom and bedroom. At the time, she thought it was a silly extravagance but now she was pretty happy that it was there. She walked over to the turret balcony, bypassing the wicker table and chairs to stand at the railing and look out at the ocean. No matter how beautiful her ocean view was, her gaze kept dropping to the jungle just below her.

She was going to have to get started on clearing the backyard soon. As she thought about how she would like her backyard to look, her mind recalled a line from Romeo and Juliet. She had just gotten out the "Oh

Romeo, oh Romeo," when she was caught off guard by a small bark.

She jerked her head to the side, surprised to find Lucky and his owner sitting on their own balcony watching her.

Max Ferris, aka the Silver Fox, lifted a glass of orange juice up in friendly greeting as his dog let out a series of excited tail-wagging barks. "You'll have to forgive Lucky. He's not used to the classics during breakfast yet."

She laughed. She knew she was being silly but she was to happy to care. She started to wave back at him when it suddenly occurred to her that she was still wearing her nightgown. She glanced down and immediately pressed a hand over her cleavage. Heat flooding her face, she muttered a quick good morning before darting back inside. She certainly didn't want to scandalize her neighbors on only the second day here. Deciding she had years to do that, she rushed around her bedroom, searching for her robe. Unfortunately, by the time she had found her robe, slipped into it, checked her reflection and stepped back outside, her neighbor had retreated inside with his dog.

Sighing in disappointment, Arden made a note to remember in the future that her private balcony wasn't so private as she made her way back into her house. She shrugged off her disappointment. It was just as well. She didn't have time to flirt with the cute guy next door. She had a lot to do today. Sometime between now and the party tonight, she was going to have to bake something that would knock her neighbors off their feet. Completely confident that one of those cookbooks she bought contained the perfect recipe, she whistled a happy tune on the way to the shower.

* * *

What seemed like a simple project, however, turned out to be far more difficult than she had anticipated.

Arden held out the book from her face and looked from the pretty frosted pink cake on the cover of her cookbook to the pink monstrosity sitting on her kitchen table. "Why don't you look like the cake in this picture?"

She glanced at the clock. She only had five hours left to come up with something for the party tonight.

She bit her lip. She didn't have to take anything. After all, Savannah did say that all she had to do was show up.

She gritted her teeth pushing such thoughts away. She wanted to make a good impression on her new neighbors. The least she could do was to come up with something edible.

She cut off a corner of the cake and took a bite, then promptly tossed the whole thing into the garbage. She didn't expect to turn into Julia Child overnight but still…

She sighed. She needed something simpler. Something she knew how to bake. Suddenly, her grandmother's famous chocolate cupcakes sprung to mind. It was always a hit at every family gathering, she thought, closing the cookbook. And if she decorated it like the cakes in the cookbooks, she bet it would get everyone's attention.

It took her ten minutes to find her grandmother's recipe buried in an old shoebox of recipes she inherited when her grandmother passed away. Making note of the ingredients, she reached for her purse and headed out to the local grocery store in town to pick up some missing items in her pantry.

Once that was done, she set off in search of the local bakery. In addition to the cakes, pies and other assortment of goodies the bakery also had a nice selection of icing kits for sale and if she had any hope of making her cake look like one of the ones in the cookbook she was going to need one of those kits. Desperately. She had half a mind to buy a cake and call it a day, but she never was a quitter.

Locking her groceries in her car, she walked down the street to the Cake Bar, a combination dessert and teashop, and stepped inside. She stopped short at the door, surprised to find Max Ferris standing at the counter.

Smiling to herself, she stepped into line behind Max as he asked the lady behind the counter if she thought he had bought enough cookies for tonight.

"Honey, you're the fourth person going to that party who's bought something from here." The woman handed him two large pink boxes. "Trust me, you have enough."

Thanking her profusely, he turned and stopped, a guilty look crossing his face as soon as he saw Arden standing behind him.

"Well, well, well, funny finding you here." Arden gestured to the boxes. "You must have quite the sweet tooth. Those wouldn't be for the party tonight, would they? You do know Savannah's expecting homemade desserts," she said in a light teasing voice.

His lips turned up at the corners. "You're here too."

She moved to a rack near the door and plucked the icing kit off the shelf. "I just came for this," she said on the way to the counter.

"Oh." He gave her a lopsided grin when she returned to his side with her purchase in hand. "Well, in my defense, I'm not the first one here today. Apparently, a couple of our neighbors showed up and bought a few items." He adopted a look of fake concern. "You aren't going to rat me out, are you?"

"Don't worry, your secret's safe with me."

The door opened and an elderly woman with snow white hair and a giant smile came bustling in. She greeted them like long lost friends, seemingly without taking a breath, as she spoke about the weather, Savannah's party, the local gossip about the mayor's race, and the fact that the Cake Bar had the absolute best cookies in the world before turning her attention away from them to the woman behind the counter.

Arden looked at the woman's back in bemusement.

"That was Emma Varner by the way," her neighbor whispered. "She works for Bruce McCallum and his granddaughter, Wendy. Nice lady but a bit on the shy side."

Arden laughed. "I could tell. I guess she's getting ready for Savannah's homemade bake off too."

"She's the one who recommended the Cake Bar to me. According to her, Savannah only expects the best. I get the feeling she's a bit particular about her parties."

"Oh? That should make tonight fun." She glanced from her the kit in her hands to the glass dessert display case. "I wonder how much that cake is."

He shook his head as he held the door open for her. "I was warned away from that one. Apparently, Duncan Thorpe picked up one just like it before I arrived."

She laughed. "Oh, for goodness sakes, is anyone baking their dessert tonight?"

"Sure." A grin lit up his face as she followed him out onto the sidewalk. "You." He popped open one box. "Want to try a cookie?"

She laughed as she took a chocolate chip cookie. She sighed as she took a bite and gooey chocolate chips hit her taste buds. "Somehow, I don't think I'm going to be impressing everyone with my dessert offering tonight."

"As long as it's chocolate I'm sure it will be delicious," Max said reaching inside the box and taking a cookie out. "It is chocolate, isn't it?"

The corners of her lips turned up as she finished off the cookie. "You'll have to wait and see."

They walked past an antique store in silence as Arden tried to think of something else to say to keep the conversation going. In desperation for something to say, she started to make some comment about the weather when he said, "So, I guess you're Sherbet."

Arden burst out laughing. "I beg your pardon?"

"Sorry, but I ran into Paige yesterday and she told me who you were."

Realization dawned. "Ah, so she finally gave my house a name. But why Sherbet?"

"I think it had something to do with the pastel pink, blue, orange and green gingerbread trim on your house." His eyes crinkled in the corners. "I think it's kind of cute. It's a lot better than my house's name."

"Oh, I don't know about that. The Silver Fox is rather nice."

His brow furrowed. "They told me they named my house Bluebeard."

Arden's eyes widened. She felt her face grow hot. "Uh, yeah. You know I think I must have been thinking of another house." She ducked her head in embarrassment, wanting to strangle Paige and Savannah.

The corners of his lips curled up but he didn't say anything for a moment. "I'm sorry about this morning," he said when the silence started to become uncomfortable. "I hope I didn't embarrass you."

She waved her hand dismissively. "No, not at all."

"I didn't mean to interrupt your soliloquy. Lucky promises to keep quiet next time."

"Well, I hate to disappoint Lucky, but that's the last performance I'll be giving on my balcony."

She was pleased to see that he looked disappointed by her statement. "I'm surprised you're going to the party. I heard you've been a no show since you've arrived."

"Well, Savannah and Paige can be rather persuasive. I wasn't avoiding them. The last couple of months have been rather hectic."

"So, what do you do for a living?"

There was a moment's hesitation. "I'm a writer. Although I don't know if I can really call myself that yet since I'm still working on my first book." His frown deepened as a worried look came into his eyes. "I have a feeling I'm going to be saying that for the rest of my life."

She glanced at him out of the side of her eye. "Writer's block?"

"Something like that." He blew out his breath. "I'm going a little stir crazy right now. You know, while I was working everyday all I could think about was retiring and getting some rest but now . . . I'm afraid I'm going a little crazy."

"I can imagine. So, what did you do before the writing bug bit you?"

There was a pause then, "Oh, a little of this, a little of that."

She frowned, surprised at his evasiveness. "A Jack of all trades?"

He grinned. "That's me."

"Sounds mysterious."

He simply shrugged.

Whatever it was he was hiding about his past, he sure seemed determined to keep it hidden.

"So, what brings you to Cloverleaf Cove?" he asked with a teasing note in his voice. "The exciting nightlife?"

She glanced around at the pretty little shops lined up in a row with friendly, happy looking people buzzing in and out. Closing her eyes, she could hear the ocean and the seagulls flying about. She could smell the clean sea air and felt a wave of peace and something she couldn't quite explain wash over her. No, excitement was not the word she'd use to characterize Cloverleaf Cove. However, she wasn't looking for excitement. A strange unsettled feeling came over her again and she frowned, wondering what it was that was bothering her.

"I've always wanted to live here," she said pushing the feeling aside. "It just seemed so peaceful."

"It seems that way," he said ominously.

She looked at him in surprise.

"Haven't you heard? This is the secret playground of the rich and famous. I have a feeling there's something seedy going on behind all these colorful shops. It seems like everyone has a deep dark secret they're desperately trying to keep hidden." At her laugh, he said, "You don't think so?"

Arden grinned. "What I think is that you've got a very vivid imagination. It's no wonder you're a writer," she said, slowing as they neared an animal hospital. A chalkboard sign announcing a Humane Society adoption event caught her attention as they passed and she paused at the window smiling down at the kittens on display.

"I think you should get one," Max said joining her at the window.

"I've never had a cat before."

"Not even when you were a kid?"

"My younger sister was allergic to animals and then as it turned out so was my husband. I never had time to take care of a pet anyways."

Max frowned. "Husband?"

"My ex-husband," she said for the first time happy to be able to describe her ex in that way. "He lives in a tiny town in Virginia now with his new wife, three cats, a dog and four step-children with another child on the way."

A little black cat with blue eyes and a white patch on her chest crawled over its siblings to get to the window. Arden smiled as the kitten stood on her hind legs and meowed up at her.

"I think you should get her."

She bit her lip. "I don't know."

"You know, I was the same as you. I never had time for a pet but then I moved here." He sighed heavily. "And frankly it can get kind of boring when you're all by yourself in one of these big rambling houses. I never noticed it before because I was always working but now with so much time on my hands . . ."

"You're lonely."

"Kind of," he admitted softly. "Which is why I picked up Lucky. He's been keeping me busy."

She chuckled. "I have no doubt."

He lightly tapped his fingers against the window. "Besides, look at her. She's practically begging you to take her. You'd break her little heart if you said no."

Arden glanced back through the window. Making a decision, she opened the door and walked inside. A little while later, she walked out carrying the kitten from the window and a bunch of supplies.

She glanced down the street to see if Max was still around, but he had disappeared again. A rumble of thunder caught her attention and she looked up surprised to see dark storm clouds approaching the town. She huddled the kitten closer to her chest as she hurried to her car.

Chapter 4

There were houses and then there were *houses*, Arden reflected as Savannah welcomed her into the Jolly Green Giant, the magnificent dark green Victorian mansion on the corner of the street.

One of the oldest homes in town, it was as venerable and imposing as its owner was. Where Arden's house was light and airy with large rooms, a multitude of windows, lace curtains and comfortable furniture, Savannah's was dark and foreboding with an old worldly feel.

As snippets of old horror movies played in her mind, an eerie feeling swept over Arden as she stood in front of the grand staircase. Antique furniture upholstered in dark green matched the heavy velvet drapes which hung from the windows, blocking out most of the light from the street lamps outside. The only windows that weren't covered were the stained glass windows on the staircase and in the downstairs hallway.

The torrential downpour, which started soon after she arrived hadn't helped to lighten the atmosphere. Great booms of thunder and flashes of lightning through the stained glass window behind her only added to the spooky atmosphere.

Despite the surroundings, her hostess couldn't have been more gracious and welcoming as she introduced her to everyone in attendance.

As they passed old family photos, Savannah regaled her with stories of Cloverleaf Cove history as well as the history of some of the leading families of the town, her family's history being the most prominent. The Harcourt family was well known in Cloverleaf Cove as community leaders, and Savannah had even joined their ranks after her husband's death.

After *Sunny and Grimes*, Savannah's wildly popular detective show, ended twenty-five years ago, Savannah retired from acting at the ripe old age of twenty-two and came home to raise her twin boys. A few more children as well as another set of twins arrived later. After her husband's death, which Savannah clearly didn't want to discuss, she threw herself into caring for her young children and eventually the town, even becoming their mayor for a brief period of time. "My daughter in law is the current mayor. You've probably seen her picture in town," she said with a wry tone of voice. "I think she's plastered her face on every lamp post in a twenty-six mile radius."

A vague image of a campaign poster appeared in Arden's mind for a brief moment, but then faded. "I'd probably recognize her if I saw her. Is she here?"

"Too busy. It's like pulling teeth to get all my kids and their spouses here at one time. My two youngest boys are a bit easier to wrangle together, but they're both doing internships this summer. I probably won't see all my children at the same time until Christmas."

"How many kids do you have?" Arden asked.

"Six."

"Wow."

Savannah shrugged. "I had to fill the rooms in this place somehow."

Arden started to laugh but then stopped, not quite sure if Savannah was joking or not. If there was one thing she learned since arriving at the Jolly Green Giant, it was that her hostess was a bit on the eccentric side. "You have a lovely house."

"Thank you. I'd be happy to give you a tour after we hand out prizes." She gestured to the grand piano where a thin red headed woman sat periodically banging a single finger against the keys. "Have you met Bruce's granddaughter, Wendy, yet?"

Arden shook her head.

"Let me introduce you then," she said leading Arden across the room. She dropped her voice low as they approached. "Wendy's a very famous author."

Arden frowned trying to remember if she had ever heard of the woman before then. "What does she write?"

"Torrid romance books. I read one of hers last year." With a light touch to Arden's arm, she paused for a moment and smiled. "I was once a very happily married woman and I still blushed."

By the time they finished winding their way around the wait staff buzzing about, Wendy had been joined by Emma Varner who was happily chatting away to the bored looking woman about the amount of calories that was sitting on the buffet table in the dining room.

Savannah politely waited until the rather talkative lady had taken a breath, before rushing in and making the necessary introductions. "Arden, I'd like you to meet Wendy Grayson and Emma Varner. Ladies, Arden took the house next door to you."

Wendy's smile was polite if not a bit disinterested as she welcomed Arden to the neighborhood. She had an air of bored detachment about her with her smile never quite reaching her eyes as she spoke. She was in her mid-to-late thirties with a thin face hidden behind large round glasses and red hair pulled back into a ponytail which hung limply down her back. She complimented Arden on her dress—a simple black cocktail dress Arden had recently picked up before she moved—in a sort of off handed way before turning and staring off into space.

Before Arden could thank her for the compliment, sincere or not, Duncan Thorpe appeared with two cups of tea in his hand that he passed to Wendy and Emma.

Wendy sighed as she took the cup, whereas Emma batted her heavily made up eyes at the man, gushing over his kindness in fetching her a cup of tea.

"I believe you know Duncan Thorpe," Savannah said when Duncan finally turned his attention away from Wendy.

Duncan nodded in greeting. "How are you enjoying your new house?"

"Quite well," Arden said with a smile. "It's everything I ever wanted."

"Well, I do hope you'll reconsider my offer. It's a shame to leave that backyard the way it is. I could fix it up really nice for you." He wrapped an arm around Savannah's shoulders. "Have you seen Savannah's yard? She finally let me get my hands on it last year and it is one of the prettiest yards in the neighborhood, even if I do say so myself. I could do something similar for you."

"Well, frankly, I still haven't quite decided what I want to do with it. Once I have it cleaned up—"

"Oh, you should talk to Julie," Emma said nodding her snow white head. "Duncan's been teaching her everything he knows."

"Julie's too busy," he said gruffly before changing the subject. "That storm outside is a beast."

Wendy snorted lightly as she brought the subject back around. "Julie's far too busy racing around town in her brand new car to work."

"She needed a new car," Duncan said defensively.

"You spoil her too much," Wendy chided. "There is no reason to spend that kind of money on her."

"Oh, I don't know," Emma said good-naturedly. "Julie's a good kid. I don't think it would hurt to spoil her once in a while."

"If she were my niece," Wendy said, "she wouldn't be getting a brand new car out of me. It's too expensive of a car for a twenty-two year old. You ought to make her work for it."

"Julie is working for it. She's going to law school in August." Duncan puffed out his chest. "Besides, I can afford it and I like spoiling her." His eyes glittered as he looked down at Wendy. "Of course, if I had someone else to spoil . . ." He offered his arm to Wendy. "Have you seen Savannah's library? She's got a first edition Edgar Allen Poe—"

Emma Varner stood up and eagerly took his arm. "No, but I'd love to see it." She chatted happily with the shocked man as she led him away from their little group.

Wendy watched them go with an annoyed look on her face before politely excusing herself.

Arden glanced at Savannah. "I don't think I've had a conversation with Duncan Thorpe that didn't seem like a sales pitch."

"Try not to take it personally. He was the same with me until I hired him to do my yard. I swear the man won't be satisfied until he's worked on every plot of ground in this town. I don't know when he's got the time. He's supposed to be working on the new park. Opening day is scheduled for next week and there's a giant gaping hole smack dab in the middle of it. I've heard that he's adding a giant fountain that cost the town a pretty penny and that no one has seen hide nor hair of the thing. It's quite the scandal."

"I'm sure," Arden said. She looked around at the people asked, "Do you throw these parties every month?"

Arden looked around in bemusement at the people milling around the house. Far more than the ten Savannah had mentioned the day before. "Do you always host these parties?"

"I try to keep these parties limited to just our closest neighbors." She sighed. "I'm afraid I don't have as much energy for large gatherings anymore. Paige usually takes over on occasion for special holidays. Christmas, Easter, Fourth of July. She keeps trying to get me to do the Halloween party." A twinkle leapt in her eye. "But for the life of me, I can't imagine why."

The front door opened and a small figure, dressed in a large black slicker, hat and boots with little yellow cartoon ducks in pink berets, stood at the door. Lightning lit up the sky behind the figure as rain blew into the foyer from outside.

Paige stomped her feet against the welcome mat. "Sorry I'm so late," she said as she juggled her hat, a bowling ball bag and a plain white box in her hands. She thrust a box towards Arden as she stepped inside.

Savannah rushed to close the door as rain splattered against her hardwood floors. She glanced down at the bowling ball bag in Paige's hands. "Honey, when I said there were going to be games tonight, I think you might have misunderstood."

Paige gave her a look as she reached in and plucked a pair of red high heels out of the bag. She sat down on a nearby bench and exchanged her boots for heels. "It's an absolute mess outside."

"Where's that handsome doctor of yours?" Savannah asked.

"In our attic." Paige slipped off her hat then shrugged out of her slicker. "Water's just pouring in."

Taking Paige's things, Savannah opened a coat closet next to the door and reached for a hanger. "What happened?"

"I don't know. Patrick's taken all my pots and pans and he's up there collecting water. I'll be glad when this rain stops." She set her boots in the closet, then took the box from Arden's hands and looked around. "So, am I the last one here?"

Just then, the doorbell rang.

Paige answered her own question with, "I guess not," as Savannah opened the door.

Bruce McCallum shook water off of his large frame like a dog, carelessly spraying water everywhere he went as he walked past the women. "Well, I'm here," he announced in a loud gravelly voice as he shrugged out of his raincoat and pushed it into Savannah's arms. "Where's my granddaughter?"

"Right here, Grandpa," Wendy Grayson said hurrying to his side. She pushed her black rimmed glasses back up onto her nose and observed her grandfather warily.

His steely gray eyes turned to her. "Forgot to mention we were having a party tonight, didn't you?"

"I didn't forget to mention it," Wendy said lightly. "You've been sick and I didn't think that you should go out in this weather." She took his arm, leading him away from the door and into the parlor. "Besides, you know how upset you get at these things."

Savannah exchanged a look with Paige as Bruce and his granddaughter disappeared from view. "Duncan's here," Savannah said to Paige. "He's been trying to get Wendy alone ever since she arrived."

Paige gave a little patty cake clap. "Oh, that's good."

"You two playing matchmaker?" Arden asked as she followed the other two women into the dining room

Paige nodded. "Duncan is in love with Wendy. They'd probably be a couple by now if it weren't for her granddad." Taking the box from Arden's hands, she turned and set it at the end of a long row of desserts. Arden rolled her eyes as soon as she saw the Cake Bar sticker on the side of the box.

Catching Arden's eye roll, Paige grinned before reaching into the box and picking up a delicious looking chocolate pie which she set on the table.

Savannah picked up a card at the end of the table and wrote Paige's name before setting the card up in front of the chocolate pie Paige brought. "I wish he and Duncan would bury the hatchet. It's not good for neighbors to be so at odds with one another. Once upon a time they used to be friends."

Checking out the desserts, Paige walked from one end of the banquet table to the other. She snuck one of Savannah's cloverleaf shaped frosted cookies off the plate and took a bite. "I don't know why Bruce bothers coming here. He never seems to have any fun."

"He does it so he can keep an eye on Wendy," Savannah said. "I feel bad for her. I remember when she and her ex-husband moved here about eight years ago.

They were such a nice couple. Always seemed happy. Then about five years ago, her grandfather had a heart attack and she invited him to stay with them until he could take care of himself. He was only supposed to stay a couple of months. He's been here ever since, and Todd and Wendy were never the same again."

"What happened to Todd?" Arden asked.

"They got divorced about a couple of months ago," Savannah said. "A few weeks after you bought your place, Todd just walked out one day. Said he had enough."

"Anyway," Paige continued, "about a month ago, we noticed that Duncan seemed to be paying Wendy a lot of attention. Smiling whenever she walked by, complimenting her on anything she did, laughing at all her jokes."

"This girl has no sense of humor," Savannah said. "That's how we knew he was in love."

Paige confirmed Savannah's remark with a nod. "We've been trying to give them more opportunities to spend time together, but whenever we start to make headway, here comes Bruce to put a stop to it."

There was a loud commotion from the foyer.

"And speak of the devil . . ." Savannah muttered as Bruce's voice carried throughout the house.

Arden followed Savannah and Paige into the foyer where Duncan and Bruce stood inches from one another while partygoers nervously hovered around.

The front door suddenly opened and Max walked in with the dessert boxes he had bought at the Cake Bar in his hands. He took one look at Duncan and Bruce, and deposited the dessert boxes on the bench by the door before wedging himself between the two angry men.

Duncan started to say something, when his niece Julie ran up to him. She tugged on his arm, pulling him away from the older man.

Bruce smiled as Duncan walked away. "That's right, run away, coward." He glared at the people standing around gawking at him. "What are you all looking at?"

Savannah crossed her arms and spoke sternly to the older man. "Bruce, we've talked about this before. If you can't behave yourself, I'm going to have to ask you to leave."

With mock horror, Bruce McCallum threw up his hands as he backed away from her. "Oh, yes ma'am, I wouldn't dream of upsetting you." He dropped his hands and started towards the parlor, his cane striking the hard wood floors with a cringe inducing thud, as he walked away. "Heaven forbid, fire and brimstone might rain down from above if I upset the great Savannah Mae Winchester."

"If you would like me to throw him out, just say the word," Max said dryly.

Savannah sighed. "If he leaves, then Wendy will leave. She doesn't get out much as it is nowadays. I would hate to see her go." She raised a questioning eyebrow as Max handed her the boxes of dessert. "Home baked?"

He gave her a charming smile. "With my own two hands."

Savannah burst out laughing. "You're such a liar. Come on in. I'll show you where the rest of the Cake Bar goodies are. It's time for the competition anyway."

The competition as it turned out was nothing more than a taste test followed by a secret vote for the most scrumptious dessert. Generous helpings of cakes, pies, cookies and fudge were sliced and handed out on china plates in short order. More than one Arden suspected came from the bakery despite the homey plates and dishes they came in.

She glanced over at Max standing nearby, turning away with a blush when he caught her looking at him. She peeked back at him under her lashes just as Bruce McCallum stepped in front of her cutting off her view.

Hooking his cane over his arm, Bruce plucked a flowered china cup off the brass bar cart next to her and poured himself a cup of Savannah's special tea.

"You're not trying any of the desserts?" she asked.

"I like to wait until the feeding frenzy is over." He pulled the cup from his lips and scowled down at the tea. "Which one's yours?"

She pointed to the miniature pink frosted cakes.

He snorted. "You baked them yourself, didn't you?"

Arden tried not to be insulted. "Of course."

He glanced at her out of the side of his eye. "Do you know Savannah Mae's big dark secret?"

Arden stiffened. She liked Savannah and she wasn't that fond of Bruce. The last thing she wanted was to hear any malicious gossip. "No, I don't and I can't say that—"

"She's part owner of that bakery in town."

Arden looked at him in surprise. "You're kidding?"

"This little 'keeping up with the Jones' game she plays is all designed to bring her money. No one bakes their own desserts. They just want to impress their neighbors and look good for Savannah." He lifted a finger to his mouth and shushed her, as Savannah looked their way.

Annabel Allen

"Well, I can't speak for everyone else," Arden said, "but I did bake my own and you should try it. You might like it."

He grumbled something unintelligible as he took a sip of tea.

"I haven't found Ivy by the way," she whispered as an aside. "Is she your cat or something?" She sincerely hoped she was a cat and not something creepy like a snake or worse. Although she couldn't imagine anything worse than a snake.

An amused look entered Bruce's watery brown eyes. "Nah, she's not my cat." He cupped his hand around the side of his mouth and whispered into her ear. "She's your roommate."

"I don't have a roommate."

"Yeah, you do." He chuckled. "You just haven't found her yet and when you do," he said adding in a sing song voice, "someone here will be in trouble."

"I really wish you'd stop talking in riddles."

He glanced at her out of the side of his eye. "How long have you been in that house? Two days now. I've been watching that house for five years, ever since Ivy went missing." He leaned closer to her, then whispered into her ear, "She kicked over a hornet's nest in more ways than one in this sleepy little town, and then poof, she was gone. I've seen some strange stuff since, especially in the last few months."

"Like what?" she asked putting some distance between them.

"Someone dressed in black digging in your yard." There was a gleam in his eye as he added, "Sometimes, he goes inside."

A shiver went up her spine. "Inside? Inside what?" she asked warily.

"In your house. I've seen him walking past the windows late at night."

She narrowed her eyes. "Who?"

"I've got cataracts in both eyes," he replied in annoyance, "I can barely see you."

He's lying, Arden thought, studying the old man. Tired of his little game, she glanced toward Savannah who was walking around the room with a top hat in her hand and collecting scraps of paper from everyone.

He grabbed her arm when she started to turn away. "I figure he's either making sure she's still there or he's moving her around for some reason. Tell you what I'll do," he said as he leaned in close once again. "I've got some money in savings, so if you find her, I might be willing to part with some of it in exchange for first dibs on her bones. I have a pretty good idea who killed her and we might be able to make ourselves a nice little profit if we knew where he buried her."

Her head whipped around. "Bones? Are you saying this Ivy person was murdered and buried in my back—?"

An angry look came in his eyes. His hand clamped down on Arden's wrist cutting off what she was about to say. "Would you stop saying her name so loudly? What are you trying to do? Get us killed too?"

Chapter 5

Bruce McCallum glanced around. Spotting Emma Varner hovering nearby, he exploded. "Why are you always spying on me? Don't you have anything better to do?" He turned back to Arden, his fingers biting into her wrist. Dropping his voice to the barest whisper, he said, "This is just between you and me, understand? If the killer knows we're on to him, he'll kill us both. You got me, Girlie?"

Arden wordlessly nodded.

He gave Emma a look of disgust before stomping away, the tip of his cane striking the floor with unnecessary force.

Emma shook her head in disapproval as he walked away. Once he was gone, she sidled closer to Arden. "Honey, don't mind Bruce. Being ornery is just his way." Her smile fell as she looked at Arden's face. "Oh, he really upset you. What did he say now?"

Arden hesitated. She was pretty sure the man was crazy, but his warning to keep their conversation silent worried her. "He was just telling me a story."

"Well, whatever it was, I wouldn't worry about it. Bruce is a born storyteller. When Wendy and her husband first hired me to look after Bruce, he tried to convince me the house was haunted. Turned out it was all a big joke of his. He had a good laugh at my expense." Spotting Duncan standing a few feet away, she called his name. "Bruce was up to his old tricks again. Tell Arden about that time he tried to convince you there was buried treasure in your backyard."

Duncan made a face. "Don't get me started. I'm so sick of that old man. He threatened to sue me yesterday."

Emma's smile fell. "What for now?"

"Alienation of affection. He's claiming that I'm turning his granddaughter against him." Duncan turned his attention to the buffet table as Savannah pulled the last piece of paper from the top hat.

"It looks like we have a tie," Savannah said smiling at Arden then Max. "Congratulations Arden! Max!" She picked up a pair of gift cards and held them up. "Welcome to the community!"

Arden blinked in surprise. "I won?"

"Newbies always win," Duncan muttered before finishing off his drink. His forehead furrowed as he looked around. "Where did Wendy go? She was just here a second ago."

Arden shrugged before joining Savannah at the buffet table.

* * *

"So, what do you plan on doing with your winnings?" Max asked her an hour later as they neared the end of their tour of the Jolly Green Giant.

They had taken a break from touring and were now in the tower room getting to know each other better while Savannah and Paige took turns peering through the telescope nearby pretending they could see the stars through the downpour outside.

Thankfully, Paige had insisted on tagging along during the tour and had found several opportunities to engage Savannah in long lengthy discussions of her home giving Arden and Max plenty of time alone. Arden couldn't have been happier. Max was not only handsome, but charming and friendly too.

She glanced at him under her lashes as he smiled down at her. She was tempted to ask him out sometime that week. After all, she was holding a twenty-five dollar gift card to the Cake Bar in her hand. How could he possibly turn her down? "I'm not sure if I should save it for a special occasion or go wild and use it all at once."

"I vote for going wild. I plan on splurging and buying one of everything with my gift card."

"Yeah, but I hate to eat alone." Licking her lips, she built up her courage to ask him out. "I'd much rather—"

The lights flickering on and off caused her to cut off the rest of her statement.

"It's all right," Savannah called out over a loud boom of thunder. "Happens all the time. Worse comes to worst we'll dig out the candles."

Everyone in the room directed their attention to the chandelier as it flickered, then went out.

"Oh rats," Savannah said from somewhere nearby. "Hang on y'all. I've got some candles in the room below us. Be right back."

Paige's chipper voice floated through the darkness. "I'll join you. You two stay right where you are. Savannah and I'll be back in about ten minutes or so."

"Oh, it won't take that lon—Ow!"

"Savannah, you best watch your step," Paige said.

"I was watching my step," Savannah complained.

The sound of their voices and high heels faded away as they walked down the spiral staircase in the center of the room.

Arden smiled in the darkness. If she didn't know better, she'd wonder if the two hadn't planned on the lights going out when they did.

"I checked the weather before I came over," Max said staring out the window. "It's not supposed to last long. It should pass over in an hour or so."

Arden murmured something about the heat, while trying to find a way to turn the conversation back to where they left off. "I hope the lights come back soon. I can barely see anything."

He returned to her side. "So, what do you think of the Jolly Green Giant?" he asked with a whisper.

"Oh, it's very lovely."

"You know her father was a mad scientist."

She laughed.

"No, it's true. I heard he had a lab downstairs where he did a lot of odd experimentations. I wonder if that's next on the tour."

"I think your imagination is working over time."

"I didn't make it up. Bruce told me all about the old man the other day. Said he was a doctor and did all sorts of freaky experiments."

"Somehow, I don't think Bruce is a reliable source."

Lightning lit up the room, casting strange shadows against the floor and causing a shiver to race down her spine. She instinctively moved closer to Max.

Feeling her body pressing up against his, he brought his arm up and draped it over the back of the couch behind her head.

The need to talk to someone about what happened downstairs and the day before bubbled up inside her. Before she could stop herself, she told Max everything that Bruce had said to her since she had met the old man.

He seemed more amused than worried. "I wouldn't take what he said seriously. Like you said, he's not a reliable source. He has a reputation around the neighborhood for tall tales. He's just trying to get a reaction out of you. I hear he does it to everyone who moves into the neighborhood."

They both looked up as the chandelier lit up above them.

She felt some of the tension leave her body. "I guess this is his version of hazing. What did he tell you?"

"Oh, let's see. Savannah's got bats in the belfry. Paige is after everyone's land so she can sell it off to some developer somewhere and make a gazillion dollars. Julie's an exotic dancer. Emma's trying to poison him. Duncan's an international jewel thief."

Arden laughed. It was hard to picture Duncan Thorpe, with his cowboy boots and outdoorsy down home manner, as a jewel thief, much less an international one. "So, Duncan's a mild manner landscaper by day and a jet setting international jewel thief by night. So, what does he think of you?"

He gave her a smug grin. "Oh, I'm a spy."

She arched an eyebrow "You are, are you?"

"Absolutely."

"Uh huh and what has he said about me?"

"He thinks you're a detective."

"Where did he get that idea?"

"Rumor has it you came into some money playing some kind of mystery game."

"Yeah, but that was just a game."

"Bruce never lets pesky things like facts interfere in his fun." He smiled. "You know what he calls Duncan, don't you? The Cloverleaf Cat Burglar."

She laughed again. "I can see that."

"Speaking of names, what did you name the kitten?"

"Clover. In honor of my new home."

"Not Sherbet?"

"Surprisingly enough, no." She glanced outside. "I hated leaving her on her first night home but at least Paige's daughter is with her. She offered to kitty sit for me."

"We're back," Savannah sang out from somewhere below the staircase. "You all ready to go back downstairs?"

Reluctantly, Arden left Max's side and walked over to the spiral staircase. "We're ready."

"I hope you two weren't too lonely without us," Paige said with a smile as she glanced from Arden to Max.

"Very funny," Arden whispered. "Where were you two?"

"Getting candles," Paige said innocently.

Arden glanced down at Paige's empty hands. "Where are they?"

Paige hid a smile and shrugged.

Shaking her head, Arden followed Paige and Savannah back downstairs.

By the time they made it to the foyer, the storm had finally tapered off to a small drizzle and for a moment, there was a mad rush as people collected their purses, umbrellas and coats, anxious to get back home before the storm clouds had a chance to let loose again.

Max gently took Arden's arm, steering her away from the large crowd near the front door and towards the library. Only a handful of people had decided to brave the weather and stay a little longer.

Duncan and Wendy were sitting in a cozy little nook in the corner. They barely glanced Arden and Max's way as they spoke to one another in low urgent whispers. Duncan's niece, Julie, meanwhile, was making herself comfortable on a nearby couch. Arden watched as the young woman kicked off her sky high heels and flopped down on the couch with a deep sigh. Seconds later, her cell phone was out and in front of her face. Emma was seated in the chair next to her, knitting what looked to be a scarf and telling some story about a previous storm that had knocked out power for a whole week.

Max took one look at the cozy group and said, "Feel like getting some more dessert?"

Arden nodded.

In the dining room, they found Bruce by the dessert table.

He pressed his fingers into Max's shoulder as they stepped into line behind him. "You tell that mutt of yours to stay out of my garden. He's been trying to dig up my begonias."

Max scowled at the older man. "It only happened once and I offered to pay you for them."

Bruce grumbled something under his breath before stepping to the side and picking up a stainless steel pie server. "Where did you all disappear too?" he asked adding an extra-large helping of chocolate pie to his plate.

"We went on a tour," Arden said, trying not to watch as he used his fingers to shovel the pie into his mouth.

Bruce's eyes turned crafty, and he leaned in close dropping his voice to a whisper. "Did Savannah show you her cellar?" he asked as he licked his fingers.

Now that she knew Bruce was nothing more than a harmless kook, Arden laughed. "That wasn't part of the tour."

He dropped the remainder of the pie onto his plate. "I knew it," he said reaching for a cupcake. "She's got something down there she doesn't want anyone to see."

"Why didn't you go and check while we were upstairs?" Max asked.

"How can I? She keeps it locked," Bruce said as though the answer were obvious. He glared at them as he picked the cupcake up with his hand and took a large bite.

Arden waited for some kind of response. She didn't really expect a compliment from the man--he didn't seem the type to hand out compliments--but she had a feeling he would make some comment.

Bruce licked the pink frosting off his fingers. "I've had worse."

"Thank you," she said in amusement as he wandered off. She smiled at Max as she placed a brownie on her plate. "I guess that was a high compliment coming from him."

Paige walked into the dining room. "Kelly called. She wanted you to know that she took your kitten back to our house."

Arden frowned at the distressed note in Paige's voice. "Is everything all right?"

"Perfect, except for the hole in my roof. She said her dad was threatening to go up there and patch it tonight. I guess I better go get my things," she said with a deep sigh as she left the room.

The grandfather clock in the foyer began to chime.

"Yeah, I guess it's getting pretty late," Max said almost reluctantly. "Now that it's stopped raining, Lucky's probably ready to go out." He lightly touched her arm, causing Arden's heart to skip a beat. "Since we're heading the same way, you want to walk together?"

She smiled in pleasure. "As long as you don't mind stopping by Paige's house to pick up the kitten."

"Don't mind at all. I can't wait to see Sherbet again."

"Clover," she corrected with a laugh as she followed him into the foyer.

She glanced at the front door surprised to find Paige staring at her boots as though she had never seen them before.

Curious, Arden walked towards her friend. "What's wrong, Paige?"

Paige looked up in surprise. She flipped the boots over and lifted them up for Arden to see. "Look."

Placing her plate onto the small round table underneath the chandelier, Arden turned and examined the muddy boots with a bemused expression on her face. "What's wrong with them?"

Paige's brow furrowed in confusion. "Well, I walked from my driveway across the street to Savannah's driveway and then I came inside."

"So?"

She shrugged as she examined the boot again. "Where did the mud come from? They weren't like this when Savannah put them in the closet. My coat hasn't dried yet either." She shook her head. "It's weird."

"Are you sure you have the right ones?"

"Positive." She slipped the boot onto her foot. "I've had these for ten years. Bought them in France at a specialty shop. I can't imagine someone else here has a pair just like them."

"Maybe someone took them thinking they were theirs." Max said. "Then realizing their mistake, they brought them back."

Paige slipped her foot into the other boot. "You're probably right. I just—" A look of alarm entered her eyes as Bruce McCallum stumbled into view. The dessert plate in his hand tilted down, sending a half-eaten piece of pie and what was left of Arden's cupcake towards the edge of the plate. Breathing heavily, his face red and sweaty, he set his plate on the table next to Arden's plate before collapsing to the ground.

They all reached Bruce's side at the same time.

"Is he all right?" Arden asked as Max pressed his fingers against Bruce's neck. The grim look on Max's face told her all she needed to know.

While Arden alerted Bruce's granddaughter, Paige called for an ambulance and then for her husband. Max, meanwhile, started CPR, trying to save Bruce's life, only stopping when Paige's husband, Patrick, arrived and took over.

A somber mood settled on the house as Patrick and the EMTs worked on Bruce. No one made a sound until Patrick sat back on his heels and shook his head.

Emma and Julie immediately burst into tears, sobbing uncontrollably as the EMTs placed Bruce on a stretcher and covered his face. Their faces grim, Max and Patrick held the door open for the EMTs before following them down the walkway.

Duncan wrapped an arm around Wendy who seemed more embarrassed than distressed by her grandfather's death. With a small smile, she apologized to Savannah as she collected her things. "What a horrible way to end the party," she said as she retrieved her grandfather's cane from the floor. "He should have never come out tonight. He hadn't been feeling well all day. I told him to just stay in bed to rest but he never listens." She lifted her hand in a wave. "Well, goodnight everyone. Again, I apologize for what happened."

"Honey," Savannah said softly, her blue eyes stricken, "there's no need to apologize."

Wendy merely smiled before turning and walking out.

Duncan wrapped his arm around his niece who was still softly sobbing. He looked over Julie's head at Emma who was standing nearby. "I think Wendy's in shock."

Wiping her eyes, Emma briefly nodded before rushing outside.

"I think I better go with you," Paige said, following Emma.

Duncan and Julie stopped at the door. He glanced back at Savannah and Arden. "Wendy just doted on her grandfather," he said softly. "I don't know how she's going to handle this."

"If she needs anything," Savannah said, "you just let us know."

Nodding, he led Julie outside.

Arden started to follow them but stopped by the little table underneath the chandelier and stared down at two plates lying there, each containing a brownie and nothing else.

"Are you okay, sugar?" Savannah asked.

"Bruce's plate is missing."

Savannah tilted her head to the side. "I beg your pardon?"

70

"Bruce's plate." Arden glanced around the large floral arrangement. "He dropped it on the table next to mine before he collapsed, but now it's gone."

Her face a mask of confusion, Savannah walked to the table. "Are you sure? There are two plates here."

Arden slowly shook her head. "He had one of my cupcakes on his plate before he collapsed but it's no longer there now. He also had part of Paige's chocolate pie on it but it's not there anymore either. What happened to it?"

Savannah looked at her with a funny expression on her face.

Suddenly, Arden felt ridiculous. Why was she making such a fuss? A man just died and here she was worrying about the contents of his plate. She smiled softly. "I guess it's not really important. I'm sorry; I'm just a bit shocked by what happened."

"Yes, but try to put it out of your mind and get some rest," Savannah said with a sympathetic note in her voice as she led Arden to the door. "We have much work to do tomorrow."

Arden stepped onto the porch with a frown. "What do you mean?"

Savannah smiled. "You'll see. Goodnight, dear."

Chapter 6

Despite Bruce's shocking death, Arden drifted off almost as soon as her head hit the pillow that night and she probably would have slept soundly through the night if it weren't for the phone waking her an hour later.

She blinked at the clock, surprised it was only a quarter to midnight and fumbled for the phone.

Lifting the phone to her ear, she closed her eyes and snuggled under the covers. "Hello?"

Paige's panicked voice came over the line. "Arden?"

"Hmm?"

"Are your doors locked?"

Arden blinked as she struggled to wake up fully. "What?"

"I don't mean to scare you but did you lock your doors tonight?"

Sleep fled as adrenaline pushed her awake. She sat up and reached for the lamp by her bed. "Yeah, of course, I did. Why? What's wrong?"

"I just found out that Kelly saw someone in your backyard tonight. That's why she came back home."

A prickle of unease caused Arden's gaze to fly to the door automatically.

Kelly's voice could be heard in the background, complaining about her mother's choice of words.

Paige sighed. "Kelly says that she *thinks* she saw someone. She's not sure. Says it could have been her imagination."

"Well, what did she see?"

There was a moment's discussion away from the phone as Paige and her daughter spoke to one another, then Kelly came on the line. "Hi, Mrs. Lynn. I didn't really see anyone. Just a shadow in your backyard. It was probably nothing."

Arden reached for Clover who was jumping over the bedding to get to her. She cuddled the kitten to her chest. "But it scared you enough to leave?"

"Well, I was watching a scary movie at the time and I guess I got a little freaked out by it. I didn't say anything because I figured it was just my imagination. I told Mom we shouldn't call. I'm sorry, we woke you."

"No, it's quite all right. Thank you for letting me know."

Paige came on the phone again. "Sorry about that, but I'd rather be safe than sorry. I guess Bruce dying like he did has made me a bit antsy tonight."

"Yeah, me too."

"I'm sure there's nothing to worry about," Paige said, clearly trying to inject a note of conviction in her voice. "It's always been safe here." There was a small pause. "I just wanted to make sure you were all right."

"I'm fine," Arden said with more confidence than she felt. "I'm glad you called."

"Well, I'll let you get back to sleep. If you need anything just call."

"Yeah, I will, thanks for calling."

As Arden replaced the phone, her attention was drawn back to the bedroom door.

Suddenly, the normal creaks and the groans of the house she had previously dismissed as nothing more than the house settling sounded far more sinister as she sat alone in her bed with only a kitten for company.

"I'm sure it's nothing," she assured Clover as she set the kitten to the side.

Another creak sent her dashing across the room and locking the bedroom door. She stood at the door for a moment before picking up her robe. "I remember being a teenager," she said to the cat as she slipped into the robe and belted it tight.

Clover hopped to the end of the bed and meowed.

"It's not like I've never gotten spooked by a scary movie before."

Turning to the nightstand, she reached for a flashlight, then walked to the French doors and stepped out onto her balcony.

The wind pushed her hair into her face and she roughly pushed it back as she peered down at her backyard. She could barely see anything. The dark storm clouds circulating above and the thick mist below worked together to obscure the ground below.

The lamps on the other side of the hedge and in her neighbors' yards provided some light at least. Enough bare patches in the hedge allowed the lamp light to spill out, lighting the far corners of the yard. However, the center of her yard was completely shrouded in darkness.

For a second, she thought she saw something move in front of the light at the back of her yard but it was impossible to see anything clearly. It would be easy to mistake a tree swaying in the wind as something else, especially if you were already scared.

That must be what happened to Kelly.

That's it.

She saw a shadow and got spooked.

Was it really so odd that, a young girl in a strange house, watching spooky movies during a thunderstorm, might become scared enough to imagine monsters in the backyard? Especially her backyard, Arden thought ruefully as her light swept over a dead tree at the back of her property. Besides, even if someone had been in her yard, they would surely be gone by now.

Just then, a shadow in the center of the yard moved, catching her attention. It changed shapes as the wind swept through, rustling the trees and causing the mist to swirl.

She turned on the flashlight and aimed its beam down at a dark shadow only just visible within the mist.

A light in Max's house appeared, followed by the sound of a door opening.

Max stepped out onto his balcony and looked at her curiously. "Lose something?"

Still training her light on the backyard, Arden walked down the length of the balcony towards Max. "Paige just called. Her daughter saw someone in my yard tonight." Her voice sounded shaky to her own ears. Silly, she thought, there was no danger. Not here. Not in Cloverleaf Cove.

She started to say something else, but stopped when her flashlight beam fell upon two glowing eyes staring back at her from the center of the yard. Instinctively, she knew it was just an animal but she still blew out her breath in relief when the eyes blinked and an owl appeared out of the mist.

She felt a laugh bubbling up as she watched the owl gracefully soar up and away. That must be what Kelly saw. She pushed her hair out of her eyes. No, there was no danger here. Just shadows.

"I'm sure everything's okay. I—" She glanced over to the side surprised to see that Max had gone back into his house.

A minute later, he reappeared at her gate with his own flashlight.

Stepping inside, she scooped Clover up into her arms, hurried downstairs and joined Max outside. She cuddled the kitten against her chest, watching as Max walked through her yard. "See anything?"

He looked up. "It's all right. There's no one out here." He stopped and trained his flashlight around the trunk of the dead tree where a group of bushes some alive, some just as dead, circled it. "If I were you, I'd be more worried about the snakes."

A shiver went down her spine. "I'm getting it cleaned up tomorrow," she vowed.

"Do you want me to check your house?"

She hesitated. It was late. He was probably tired and she was feeling a bit silly for making such a fuss but . . . She glanced back at her house as Max joined her on her porch. Kelly had left the doors unlocked when she left.

A memory of Bruce whispering in her ear came to her just then.

Someone dressed in black digging in your backyard. Sometimes, he goes inside.

Max cleared his throat. "You know, I think we'd both sleep better if I checked it out," he said gently.

Arden nodded wordlessly as she led him into the house. She stayed in the kitchen with Clover as he made a sweep of the downstairs.

She was pleased to see from her vantage point by kitchen counter that he was thorough. Every door was opened, and every dark corner investigated thoroughly before he moved upstairs and then after a while back down and into the basement.

When he was done, he returned to her side.

"All clear."

She felt a bit of tension leave her body. "That's a relief."

"If I were you, I'd lock the door and then get some sleep. I'm not far away, so if anything happens, just yell and I'll come running."

"If you are able to hear me," she blurted out, somewhat surprised by her own cynicism.

His eyes softened. "I'll hear you." He reached out and rubbed his thumb underneath Clover's chin. She purred happily, stretching out her neck to rub her head against his palm. "Even if I didn't hear you, Lucky would. Don't worry. Everything's fine," he said before saying goodnight and stepping outside.

He waited on the other side of the door for her to lock it, and then with a wave, he turned and moved swiftly through the backyard towards the gap in the hedge between their houses.

Once he was gone, Arden walked from window to window checking each lock. When she came to the library, she stopped at the front window. Underneath the porch light, directly in front of the window were a pair of muddy boot prints that hadn't been there earlier that day.

Her first thought was that the footprints belonged to Max, but then dismissed that idea. He never stepped a foot on her porch.

Setting Clover on the floor, she slipped through her front door and out onto her wraparound porch. Spotting a pair muddy footprints, she followed the steps around the side of her house, only stopping when a bright pink flower caught her eye. She brushed the mud off the flower and held it up to the porch light. Standing, she moved to the railing and swept her flashlight around. There were a dozen or so white and purple flowers on her side of the yard and a few scraggly yellow bushes next to Wendy's house but no pink flowers anywhere as far as she could see.

She swept her light along the side of her house towards the gap in the hedges leading to her backyard.

She trained her flashlight on another pink flower, floating in the muddy puddle in front of the gap.

Automatically, she thought the intruder must have come in this way.

Out of the corner of her eye, she noticed a pair of glowing eyes staring at her from behind her library window and she whirled around, her heart pounding in her ears.

She blew out her breath in relief as Clover meowed at her from the windowsill. "Clover, you scared me half to death, baby."

Clover meowed again.

A strange feeling swept over Arden suddenly, as the hair on the back of her neck stood up. She couldn't explain ir, but she suddenly got the feeling that she was being watched.

She glanced over towards Bruce and Wendy's purple house, her gaze slowly moving up past one dark window after another, searching for the source of her unease.

A shiver snaked down her spine as a pair of curtains on the top floor moved and the sliver of light spilling out between them was extinguished.

Chapter 7

Murder, that was what it was, Arden thought the next morning as she sat on her balcony with Clover on her lap and a cup of coffee in her hand. She had spent a sleepless night tossing and turning, jumping at every little sound she heard until she finally got up got dressed and sat down on her balcony to watch the sunrise. She wasn't sure when she decided that Bruce had been murdered, but at some point during the night, she came to the realization that he had with a sickening sort of dread.

Too many strange little things had happened during the night. Paige's muddy boots and wet coat, the intruder sneaking through her yard during a storm, Bruce's shocking death and someone switching out his plate for another while he lay dying were just too unsettling to ignore.

Why would anyone take Bruce's plate and replace it with another? It was ridiculous. There was no reason to switch it out unless there was something wrong with it. Something someone didn't want anyone else to find.

Poison.

That was the only answer she could think of. Someone had poisoned him. Whoever killed Bruce replaced his poisoned desert with a harmless brownie while everyone's attention was diverted.

Clover stretched out on Arden's lap for a second before turning and rubbing her head against Arden's hand. Arden petted the kitten, scratching one ear until she settled back down on her lap. Almost immediately, her thoughts drifted back to Bruce.

Bruce had warned her it would happen last night. What had he said? Something about how if the killer knew . . .

Her fingers curled into a fist. The killer must have overheard them talking. She closed her eyes trying to think back to that moment. There were so many people in the room that night, crowded around the dining room like sardines. Bruce had caught Emma standing nearby but did he know Wendy, his granddaughter, was standing right behind him, or that Duncan was right next to her?

Arden saw them and didn't think anything about it at the time. Did they hear her mention Ivy's name? It wasn't as if she was whispering when she said the girl's name.

Bruce's words came back to her then as clear as though he was standing right next to her.

If the killer knows we're on to him, he'll kill us both.

Bruce died soon after.

She opened her eyes as a horrible thought occurred to her. What if she were next. What if the killer had left the party last night just to scope out her house, and get the lay of the land before making his next move?

Checking over both shoulders, she quickly reminded herself that Bruce was a very sick man in mind and body. He seemed to get a kick out of upsetting people. Ivy might not even exist outside his imagination. It could just be a coincidence that he died not long after making up a story to frighten her.

She nodded to herself. There could be a reasonable explanation for Paige's missing boots and the intruder Kelly had seen in the backyard.

Besides, she thought, returning her attention to the ocean, the killer, if there is one, wouldn't need to scope out her house.

Sometimes, he goes inside.

She tipped her head back with a groan as bits and pieces of Bruce's crazy story came back to her.

Sighing, she scratched underneath Clover's chin. "Well, there's an easy way to prove whether Bruce was telling the truth, isn't there, Clover?"

Clover answered her with a deep purr, and then a meow of protest as Arden stood up. Anxious to put her mind at ease and prove Bruce was just making things up, Arden made her way downstairs with Clover scampering behind her. The hair on her neck stood up as she walked through the silent house. She looked over each shoulder before hurrying into the library and shutting the door. She slid into the chair behind her desk and turned on her computer.

A quick internet search of her address and the name Ivy turned up one result. A five year old newspaper article about a local theft. According to the article, Ivy Kent, the Oakley's live-in housekeeper, allegedly caused over ten thousand dollars in damage and stole thousands of dollars' worth of jewels and cash while Gladys and Ted Oakley were celebrating their fiftieth wedding anniversary on the Serenity of the Seas. The article ended by mentioning that there was a warrant out for Ivy's arrest.

Arden attempted several more searches, but other than that one article, there didn't appear to be anything else written about the theft or Ivy Kent.

She sat back with a sinking feeling in her stomach.

Bruce was telling the truth about one thing at least. Ivy was real and she did live in this house.

The question was, did she run away like the article said or was Bruce right, and she was still here—Arden's gaze swept over the walls of her house—somewhere?

The grandfather clock in the hallway chimed causing her to jump.

Oh, get hold of yourself, Arden, she thought to herself. No one's going to jump out of the shadows. You're perfectly safe.

Perfectly safe.

Perfectly alone.

She ran her hands down her arms.

What she wouldn't give to have someone else in the house right now. Someone nice and friendly.

A soft meow drew her attention to the floor.

She smiled down at the kitten. "Well, at least I have you," she said scooping Clover up into her arms. "You'll protect me, won't you?"

Clover answered her with a deep-throated purr.

She cuddled the kitten to her chest as she walked back upstairs. Aware of the stillness of the house, she showered and dressed in record time, then hurried back downstairs.

She needed a plan, she thought as she dragged out her new cookware. The first thing she usually did when starting any mystery game was to gather as much information about the people she was playing with as quickly as she could. However, how was she going to get it without tipping off the killer that she was investigating? The mere mention of Ivy's name, may have gotten Bruce killed. Arden wasn't in any hurry to stamp a bullseye on her back if there wasn't already one there.

She shook her head. What was she doing? This wasn't a mystery game. This was real. Did she really want to get involved?

She glanced over at the jungle. Did she have a choice? She had a feeling that the killer was watching her now, waiting to see what she would do.

She was going to have to be very careful.

With that sobering thought, Arden reached into the refrigerator and began pulling out the ingredients for her mother's famous breakfast casserole.

An hour and half later, she carried the casserole next door to the purple house.

Emma Varner, her eyes red and overflowing with tears, welcomed Arden inside with a grateful smile.

While slightly larger than her own home, Bruce and Wendy's home boasted the same beautiful architecture but where her house was light and airy, theirs was dark and claustrophobic.

Arden had a feeling the dark purple drapes and faded gray wallpaper had something to do with the sad almost melancholy atmosphere but she couldn't lay all the blame on the decorations. When poor Emma Varner wasn't bravely trying to hold back her tears, she was sobbing uncontrollably.

Arden did her best to comfort the woman but the only thing that seemed to dry her eyes was the subject of Wendy and the fact that Emma hadn't seen her cry once since her grandfather died.

"I just don't understand it," Emma said as she took the casserole and carried into the small and rather utilitarian kitchen. "It's like she doesn't even care that he's dead. If I didn't know better I'd think she was happy he was gone."

"Perhaps she's still in shock," Arden offered diplomatically. "I don't know her, of course, but she seems to be a rather reserved woman. She might be the type to save her grief for when she's alone."

Emma's mouth trembled slightly as fresh tears appeared in her eyes. "Here, come and see." She motioned for Arden to follow her upstairs. Arden reluctantly followed, feeling as though she was intruding as she walked back through the house towards the dark staircase in the foyer. She glanced at the chairlift sitting unused at the bottom of the stairs and felt a sense of sadness.

"Come on," Emma said in a choked voice. "It's up here."

They walked up to the attic floor and to a small bare bedroom, its single bed stripped of covers.

Emma's face crumpled as she gestured to the room. "Wendy's already packed away his things. She put them all into boxes and carried them out to the shed." She reached into her pocket, pulled out a tissue, and pressed it to her eyes.

Arden's heart broke for the older lady. Despite Bruce's gruff manners, it was clear the woman cared for the old man and was grieving. She reached out and touched Emma's arm.

Emma smiled sadly, as she patted Arden's hand. "I just can't believe he's gone." With one last pat of Arden's hand, she walked to a small bathroom in the corner of the room.

Arden opened the French doors and stepped out onto the balcony. Two rocking chairs, facing away from each other, sat at each end of the balcony. A pair of binoculars sat on the rocking chair facing her house.

Perfect view of the ocean, she thought as her gaze dropped down to the right, noting Bruce also had a perfect view of her backyard as well as Duncan's. She stepped back inside, her gaze falling to the window by the bed.

Arden pushed aside the curtain. "Was Wendy up here last night?" she asked as Emma stepped out of the bathroom.

Emma tore her tissue into two. "No, she went to bed as soon as we came home. She packed everything away this morning before she left to go to the funeral home."

"I thought I saw someone at this window about midnight last night."

Emma's shook her head. "You must have been mistaken." Tears spilled over as she looked around with a heartbroken expression on her face. "It's like he was never even here. I think—"

The sound of the doorbell cut off whatever she was about to say. Ushering Arden out, Emma closed Bruce's door and hurried down the stairs.

Duncan was waiting at the door with a somber expression on his face.

After warmly greeting Emma with a hug, he asked, "Is Wendy ready?"

"She's at the funeral home," Emma said, brushing away the evidence of her tears and forcing a smile to her face.

Duncan frowned. "Now? She called an hour ago and asked me to go with her. Why didn't she wait for me?" When Emma couldn't give him an explanation, he sighed heavily and pulled out his cell phone. "I better call her and see if she's still there." He quickly dialed a number, and then held the phone up to his ear. "Wendy, I thought you were going to wait for me," he said as he stepped down the hallway and slipped through a pair of double doors.

"I'm sorry about last night," Emma said, sniffling. "I just hate that Bruce was being so nasty to you. He wasn't always like that, but sometimes, he could get in a mood."

"It's all right," Arden assured her.

Emma primly folded her ripped tissue in half. "No, it isn't. He shouldn't have acted that way. I guess he was just feeling poorly and decided to take it out on everyone else." She cocked her head to the side. "What was he telling you about Ivy? Something about something being buried?"

Arden froze, because that meant Emma *was* listening in on their conversation last night.

Almost by instinct, Arden's sense of self-preservation overshadowed her innate honesty. "Buried? Goodness, no. No, that's not what we were talking about at all."

Emma's eyes widened. "Then what were you talking about?"

An uncomfortable silence began to build as Arden searched for something to say. "I was just asking about the people who used to live in my home and he mentioned something about an Ivy something or other living there, but that was it."

Duncan appeared in the hallway just then with a scowl on his face. "Ivy? What's this about Ivy?" he asked as he pocketed his phone.

"Arden asked Bruce about her," Emma helpfully added.

"No," Arden said quickly raising her finger to make her point. "No, I *did not* ask about Ivy. I didn't ask about Ivy at all." She backed up to the door, fumbling with the handle. The longer she stood there, the more she felt like a mouse caught between two cats.

Duncan crossed his arms. "What did he tell you that got you so upset last night? Did he say something about Ivy?"

"Ivy? No, of course not." Where was that door handle? Arden thought frantically, her fingers reaching out behind her, searching for the handle. "Wh-why would Bruce say anything about Ivy? I didn't know her. I don't know anything about her actually."

Emma's brow furrowed. "Sweetie, what's wrong?"

"Nothing," Arden said with a laugh.

"Why are you acting so nervous?" Duncan asked.

"I'm not nervous—" Arden let out a little scream of surprise as the door suddenly hit her in the back and propelled her forward.

Duncan caught her before she could fall. "Are you all right?"

"I'm fine," she said bolting out of his arms.

He glanced towards the door with a sigh. "Julie, you almost knocked Arden down. What are you doing barging in like that?"

His niece blushed. "Oh, my gosh. I am so sorry. I didn't hurt you, did I?"

Arden tucked her hair behind her ears as she gave Duncan and Emma a wide berth. "No, I'm fine. Just fine."

"Well," Duncan said with an annoyed sigh, "whatever Bruce told you to get you all upset last night, just forget it. He was just messing with you, which reminds me," he added, turning his attention to his niece, "Julie, Arden needs someone to help mow her lawn. I told her last night that you'd be happy to help her."

"Oh," Julie said in surprise. "Okay." She turned to Arden. "When would you like me to start?"

"How about now?" Arden asked backing out the door. No time like the present.

* * *

"Are you sure you don't want some sweet tea, Julie?" Arden raised her voice to be heard over the sound of the lawn mower as she walked over her freshly mowed backyard with a glass of iced tea in one hand and Clover in the other.

Julie Thorp turned off the mower and eagerly reached for the glass. While she gulped it down, Arden took a moment to look over her backyard. It seemed bigger now that the grass had been cut. Julie handed the glass back, then swiped her forearm across her mouth. "Almost finished," she huffed as she returned to the mower.

Arden smiled. Julie was definitely a hard worker. Quick and efficient, she tackled the backyard as if she was on a mission or a deadline, only stopping when Arden insisted the girl have lunch. She scarfed down the lunch, and then quickly returned to the yard, alternating between clearing dead, broken tree limbs, pruning out of control bushes and mowing down the overgrown grass.

Just watching Julie as she worked was making Arden tired, but she wasn't about to stop her.

She could already tell that the yard was going to be beautiful once Arden figured out what to do with it. She walked around, something she had avoided doing while the grass was so tall, taking stock of the length of the yard and the bushes and plants that were there. As she passed by one of the crepe myrtles, she spotted a bush with familiar looking pink flowers nearby and stopped.

When Julie was finished, she walked over to where Arden was standing. She wiped an arm across her sweating forehead. "Do you want me to do the front yard now?"

"Sure." Arden glanced up as a wasp flew into view. She held Clover's paw down as the kitten reached up to swat at the buzzing annoyance. "I can't thank you enough for coming out on such short notice."

"No problem, but I'm surprised you didn't ask my uncle."

"Well, to be honest, I did," Arden admitted. "When I told him that all I wanted was someone to mow for me, he suggested I contact you."

Julie grunted. She started to turn away but stopped and sighed. "Can I ask you a personal question?"

Arden nodded.

"Why didn't you let Uncle Duncan finish the backyard? Were you not happy with him?"

"No, I was very happy. I just wanted a little project to keep me busy." She blew out her breath as she looked at the size of the yard. "I may have bitten off more than I can chew." She smiled. "To be honest, I'm not exactly known for my green thumb. I haven't the slightest idea where to begin."

For a moment, she considered calling Duncan Thorp and having him work on the back, but she pushed the thought away. Duncan's salesmanship and then his abrupt dismissal when he realized she wasn't going to hire him to work on her backyard annoyed her. Besides, his proposed plans for her backyard were far too complicated for her tastes. "I just want something simple and pretty. Something fitting for the house. Maybe a seashell walkway like the one out front leading to the back gate and a fountain in the center." She glanced back down at the bush. "Maybe some roses. Some white wicker furniture might be nice. I've seen old pictures of Victorian gardens and I think I would like something like that."

Julie turned her attention to the yard, her intelligent brown eyes roving from one end to the other. "You know, I could help you." Excitement colored her voice as she turned toward Arden. "I wouldn't charge as much as my uncle and I could whip your yard into shape in no time. I'd do whatever you want. I know the owner of the local nursery and he said he'd give me a deal whenever I asked."

Arden tilted her head as she regarded the young woman. She could hear the desperation in her voice and frowned. "Have you ever done any landscaping?"

She nodded. "I've been helping my uncle since he took me in after my dad died. Trust me. I know I can give you exactly what you want."

"Your uncle has been pushing me to give him my business. Won't he be upset with you if I give it to you?"

Worry came into the girl's eyes. "Maybe but . . ." She blew out her breath in defeat. "He's already upset with me, so I can't imagine it could get any worse."

"Why? What happened?"

"Uncle Duncan doesn't have faith in me," Julie admitted softly. "He treats me like a kid."

"Oh, I'm sure that's not true."

"He still calls me Cinderella." She sighed. "I can't seem to convince him that I'm an adult now and that I'm perfectly capable of doing this job." She waved a hand out towards the yard. "I've been watching him for the last six years and have learned so much from him. All I want to do is apply what I've learned. Meanwhile, he's been begging his two sons who live all the way in Arizona and only visit during the holidays to come out here and work for him. For goodness sake, they kill everything they touch."

Arden laughed.

"I'm serious. They can't even keep a cactus alive." She pressed her hands together and began to beg. "Please. Please. Please. If I could prove to him that I'm just as good—that I can do this—I know he'll let me work with him."

Arden lifted her hands to halt the girl's pleading. "Okay, okay, I'll give you a chance."

Julie threw herself towards Arden wrapping her in a giant bear hug. "You won't regret this." Suddenly, Arden found herself being taken on a tour of her own yard, as Julie began peppering her with question after question. What are her favorite flowers? What about her favorite colors? Was she interested in a fountain? A pool? Any allergies? Julie retrieved a notepad out of the kitchen and wrote down each answer. When she had wrung as much information about Arden's likes and dislikes as she could, she flipped the paper over and began sketching the dimensions of the yard.

While Julie worked on her sketch, Arden walked around her newly mowed yard with Clover at her side. She paused again at the bush with the pretty pink flowers, her thoughts going back to the night before.

She plucked a pink bloom off the bush and held it up to her nose. Just how did this little flower get all the way over to her porch? The killer obviously must have carried it over when he snuck back out of her yard, but what was he doing out here in the middle of a storm in the first place?

Dropping the bloom, she walked around the bush and frowned at a section of turned up dirt. Something white sticking up out of the ground caught her attention and she knelt down to investigate. She pushed away grass clippings, dried leaves and twigs away to reveal a large piece of bone china sticking up out of the ground. She pulled the piece out of the dirt and set it aside. Then, very carefully, she began digging at the loose dirt only stopping when Julie suddenly shouted no a few minutes later. She turned just in time to see Julia scoop Clover up and pull the pink flower Arden had discarded away from the kitten's paws. "You better be careful, baby."

Thinking that Julie had spotted a snake, Arden stood up and nervously looked down at her feet. "Why? What happened?"

Julie held up the pink bloom she had taken from Clover. "She was playing with the oleander." At Arden's blank stare, Julie added, "It's poisonous."

Arden stared down at the pink bloom. "Poisonous?"

"Very. It's pretty, but if I were you, I'd get rid of it, especially if you're going to have pets."

The piece of china forgotten for a moment, Arden reached for her kitten. "Is she all right? Do you think she ate any?"

"No, I was watching her pretty closely. She was just playing with it." Julie glanced down at the small hole Arden made in the dirt, automatically reaching into her back pocket and pulling out her notepad. "Do you want to plant something here?"

"No," Arden said bending forward and picking up the piece of china that she had found. "I just found this in the dirt and was wondering if there were more pieces like it." She ran her thumb over the small purple flowers on the china. "Do you know what this used to be?"

Julie tilted her head to the side as she examined the piece. Finally, she said, "No, but I remember Mrs. Oakley had drapes that color purple. Ugliest things I ever saw. She loved those drapes though," she said over her shoulder as she wandered away.

Arden started to put the china back down again when she noticed a long strand of blonde hair hanging from a crack in the china.

A sick feeling began to take hold as Arden turned her attention to the plot of ground behind her.

Just big enough for a body.

"Julie, did you know Ivy Kent?"

Julie looked up as she jotted down something on the notebook in her hand. "Sure, she used to live here for a while."

"Was she blonde?"

"Yeah, I mean it came from a bottle, but sure." Julie frowned. "How do you know Ivy?"

Arden kicked a mound of dirt over. "I looked up my house online and saw a newspaper article about her. It said she stole some things from the Oakleys."

Julie made a face. "Yeah, Ivy got into some trouble around here and had to skedaddle," she said reluctantly. "It was a huge scandal."

"Did she really steal all that stuff?"

Julie took a deep breath before letting it out slowly. "I guess so. She had . . . issues." Clearly hoping to change the subject, she held out the notepad and proudly presented her sketch. "This is what I'm thinking we should do. Now, I know it doesn't look like much, but I'm just going to finish up mowing, and then I'm going to go home and write up a formal proposal." A brilliant smile lit up her face. "This is so exciting. I can't wait to show you my plan for your yard. I'll email you tonight. Would that be okay?"

"Yeah, that would be great," Arden glanced back at the ground, "but first, do you think you could find a shovel for me?"

* * *

Arden dropped her shovel on the ground and sat down next to the oleander bush. Might as well stop, she thought taking a deep breath. The sun had gone down and it was getting too dark to see. Not that there was much to see. The only thing she had uncovered during her afternoon of digging was dirt, sand and rock. No other pieces of bone china or bones of any kind turned up during her digging. She didn't know whether to be relieved or disappointed.

What was she thinking? Did she actually expect to find a dead body?

She kicked over a rock with the toe of her tennis shoe, making a mental note to have Julie add lights to her design for the backyard the next time she saw her. Maybe along the pathway she wanted leading to the gate.

"Arden," Paige's voice called out from somewhere nearby. A second later, she appeared on the dirt path near the sunroom. "Arden, are you back here?"

"Over here, Paige."

Paige stepped out onto the grass and looked around. "Wow, what a big difference a little mowing makes. I think—" Her gaze landed on Arden. "What in the world are you doing?"

Arden looked up at Paige, one of three people on her street that she was certain she could trust and said, "I'm searching for a dead body."

Paige tilted her head. "I'm sorry, a what?"

"A dead body."

"Oh." Paige frowned. "Are you feeling all right?"

"I'm perfectly fine."

Paige lifted her hands up in a shrug. "Well, you've got my attention. What's going on?"

"Do you remember hearing about a girl by the name of Ivy Kent?"

Paige thought about it for a moment. "The name doesn't ring a bell. Why?"

"She used to live here." Arden dusted her hands off and stood. "I need to find someone who knew her and is willing to talk about her. Savannah's lived here her whole life, hasn't she? She must remember her. Do you know where she is right now?"

"Not at the moment, but she'll be at my house an hour from now. Patrick and the kids are going to a ballgame tonight and I thought I might throw a little dinner together for just us girls. Would you like to come?"

"I would love to. I'm absolutely starving."

Paige nodded sagely. "Well, I'm not sure, having no experience with it myself, but I would expect digging holes in the backyard looking for dead bodies would work up quite the appetite."

Chapter 8

"Oh, it was definitely murder," Savannah said when the topic of conversation had moved to Bruce McCallum's death.

Arden had refrained from mentioning her suspicions during dinner but couldn't resist after they moved to Paige's cozy screened in gazebo at the front of her house to enjoy a piece of chocolate pie. With a direct line of sight to Savannah's house, Arden could think of nothing but Bruce's death the night before.

Savannah helped herself to another after dinner mint from the candy dish on the table. "I'm missing one dessert dish," she said in an ominous tone of voice.

Paige looked at her in exasperation. "Savannah, be serious. Someone probably set it down somewhere and you just haven't found it yet. It doesn't mean Bruce was murdered." Ever since Arden told the other two women of her suspicions, Paige had tried her best to set their minds at ease. "Bruce was an old man. It was just his time to go."

Savannah waved her hand dismissively. "Nonsense. He was murdered. I've thought it ever since Arden told me about the missing plate."

"Why would someone murder Bruce and then steal your plate?" Paige asked.

Savannah smiled sweetly. "Darling, obviously, they wanted to get rid of the evidence." Her eyes twinkled under the string of lights above their head with undisguised glee. "Which can only mean one thing."

"Bruce was murdered," Arden added softly.

Savannah nodded. "Yes, that's correct." She picked up the china teapot in the center of the white wicker table and poured herself another cup of tea. "But why kill Bruce? He was ornery but that's certainly no reason to kill a man."

"He knew something he shouldn't have," Arden said. "And I think the killer poisoned him to keep him quiet."

Paige sighed. "Arden, he had a heart attack."

"I have an oleander bush in my backyard," Arden said. "I looked up the effects this afternoon. It can mimic a cardiac arrest."

Savannah sat up straighter. "Why do you think the killer used oleander?"

Arden dropped her voice to a whisper. She wasn't sure why she felt she needed to whisper. Paige's home was far enough away from the other houses on the street that she doubted anyone could overhear them, but just the same, she lowered her voice. "Kelly was pet sitting for me last night. She went home early because she thought someone was in my backyard, and then later that night, I found an oleander bloom and some muddy footprints on my porch on the other side of the house."

A look of concern crossed Paige's face at the mention of her daughter. "What are you saying?"

Arden blew out her breath before adding, "I think that while we were upstairs in the tower room someone stole your boots and slicker and then ran over to my house to grab the oleander. I think that's what startled Kelly."

"If so," Savannah said, "the killer had to have come to my house before it started raining. Everyone who arrived later had their own raincoats, boots or umbrellas. Why else would the killer need to borrow someone else's?"

"Do you remember who arrived before the rain started?" Arden asked.

Savannah looked thoughtful. "Duncan and Julie were first. Wendy and Emma arrived a few minutes later. Then you came. It started pouring soon after you arrived. All the ladies were wearing high heels and Duncan wore cowboy boots."

"We can probably rule Duncan out then," Arden said.

"We could rule him out anyway," Paige said with an arched eyebrow. "There's no way he could fit into my boots."

Savannah lifted a finger. "I'm not so willing to rule him out. Duncan is madly in love with Wendy. I've felt for a long time that the only thing keeping those two lovebirds apart was Bruce. Your muddy boots may be a red herring. Perhaps, they were muddy when you placed them into the closet."

"My boots were not muddy," Paige said defensively. She shook her head. "Come on, ladies, this is silly. We all had dessert that night. None of us died or got sick."

"Well, not everything was poisoned," Savannah reasoned. "Only one piece of dessert was and that piece was given to Bruce. The killer must have put the poison in the frosting of the cupcake."

Arden grimaced. The idea of her dessert being used to deliver the poison didn't sit well with her. She dug her fork into the pie and examined it with a frown. "What about the chocolate pie?"

"What about it?" Paige asked warily.

"I watched Bruce practically shove a huge piece into his mouth before he died," she said setting her fork back down on the plate. "Maybe it was poisoned."

Paige pushed away her plate of pie with a disgusted look.

"I doubt it would have taken much poison to kill him," Savannah continued with a gleam in her eye. "Bruce was not a well man. He had a list of aliments a mile long. It probably just took a little to push him over the edge."

"I think you've both lost your mind." Paige laughed nervously. "The man was sick. Wendy had even been looking into funeral arrangements for the last few months."

Savannah gave Arden a meaningful look over her teacup. "Well, isn't that coincidental."

"How do you know she was making funeral arrangements?" Arden asked. "Did she tell you that?"

"No, I saw her coming out of the funeral home a couple of months ago." Paige looked at them both in exasperation. "For goodness sakes, the man was pushing ninety and had suffered several near fatal attacks in the past ten years. I'd be surprised if Wendy hadn't been looking into funeral arrangements." Paige's aversion to her own pie seemingly melted away as she reasoned with them. Reaching for her fork, she took a large bite before adding, "I don't see why someone would go to all the trouble to poison him. There must be better ways to kill a man without anyone suspecting. As soon as they do an autopsy—"

Savannah shook her head. "They only do an autopsy if they suspect murder." Her voice hardened. "I spoke to the sheriff this morning and he refuses to investigate." She rolled her eyes. "Apparently, a missing dessert dish is not enough evidence."

Paige's eyes widened. "You spoke to the sheriff? Have you lost your mind?"

"What about this?" Arden leaned forward once again dropping her voice to a whisper. "Bruce told me that he saw someone digging in my yard. Not once but several times. If we told the police that, maybe then they'll do something."

Savannah snorted. "Hardly. Everyone knows Bruce couldn't see five feet in front of his face."

"No," Arden said, "but Kelly saw someone in my yard last night. She couldn't tell anything about him but it scared her enough to send her running back home. Maybe that would be enough to convince them."

Savannah crossed her arms. "The sheriff seemed convinced I was off my rocker when I told him of my suspicions. I doubt a teenage girl seeing shadows in the backyard is going to somehow convince him he's wrong."

They fell silent for a moment, each lost in thought.

"But why?" Paige asked. "Who would want to kill Bruce?"

"Anyone who's ever met him?" Savannah pondered.

"Last night," Arden said, "Bruce made me an offer. He said that if I found Ivy's body he'd pay me."

Savannah's eyebrows rose. "Ivy? As in Ivy Kent?"

"I think so. He said that he had a pretty good idea who murdered her and that if we found her body maybe it would be worth something to her killer. I think her killer

101

overheard us. Emma definitely heard us. She confronted me about it this morning. Duncan and Wendy were standing behind Bruce at the time. They may have been listening in on our conversation too. What if that's what got Bruce killed? What if . . ." Not wanting to voice her fears, she turned away.

Paige frowned. "You think someone's after you now?"

"No," Arden said quickly. "At least not . . . yet."

Paige bit her lip as a worried look came in her eye. She turned to Savannah. "Who is this Ivy person Bruce mentioned?"

Savannah set her teacup down. "She used to work for the Oakley's. Live in help. About five years ago, they went on a month long cruise to celebrate their fiftieth wedding anniversary and left Ivy at home alone."

"What happened?" Arden asked.

"Nothing good," Savannah replied. "She was young, pretty and completely irresponsible. A few days after they left, she threw a party and apparently trashed the place. Someone got hold of the Oakleys who promptly fired her over the phone. They called the police from Bermuda or someplace like that, but before the police could arrest Ivy, she took off. No one has seen her since."

A flicker of doubt began to appear in Paige's eyes. "That doesn't mean she's dead. Someone had to have seen her leaving at least."

Arden nervously played with the bracelet at her wrist. "I'm starting to wonder if she left at all."

Paige pursed her lips together. "Maybe if we find this Ivy person we can prove to you that Bruce wasn't murdered and no one is after you."

"Great! I hope you do," Arden said. "I hope Ivy Kent is alive and happy as can be. I would be thrilled if that were true."

Paige nodded to herself. "Then that's what we'll do."

Arden glanced out down the street towards the pretty gingerbread houses framed in a soft glow of lights. Everything looked so peaceful and innocent.

Pretty doll houses all in a row.

Arden laughed self-consciously. "If we could find Ivy, I could stop digging up my yard looking for a dead body."

"I doubt you'll find anything there," Savannah said. "If I had buried a body in someone else's backyard, I'd make sure I'd move it before the new owners came in and started digging things up."

"Did Ivy have any enemies?" Arden asked. "Anyone who would want to kill her?"

Savannah pushed her piece of chocolate pie around with her fork. "She worked for Wendy before she took the job with the Oakleys. Wendy hired her to help take care of the house after Bruce moved in. She quit a month later."

"Why?"

"She told me that she didn't like the way Wendy's husband, Todd, was looking at her. She didn't have very nice things to say about Wendy either, but then, Wendy was always accusing her of something or other." Her brow furrowed. "I remember there was something strange going on between Duncan and Ivy as well. I saw them arguing with one another during one of my parties a few days before she disappeared. I don't know what it was about but Ivy was angry about something." She folded her arms on the table and leaned forward. "There's something else I remember too. A friend of Ivy's came by a few months after she left looking for her. Seemed surprised when we told him that she had left. He wasn't so much surprised that she had stolen somethings from the Oakleys or she had a warrant out for her but he was surprised she didn't come to him for help. Said she had always come to him whenever she got into trouble. He was always the first person she would contact when something went wrong."

Paige shivered despite the warm night air. "You two are scaring me, you know that?" She lowered her voice. "Do you honestly think one of our neighbors is a murderer?"

Arden met Savannah's eyes over the table.

"Yes, we do," Savannah answered for her. "Now, the question, ladies, is just what are we going to do about it?"

Chapter 9

First thing the next morning, Arden set off for town. With Paige and Savannah's help, she had come up with a plan of attack. She figured that if they could prove that Ivy was dead and that Bruce knew, perhaps the police would take them seriously enough to order an autopsy. Once the police had proof that Bruce was poisoned, she figured they could then step back and let the authorities handle the rest.

With that in mind, they each came up with goals they hoped to accomplish before they met again.

Savannah was going to talk to her daughter-in-law the mayor, in the hopes that she could use her position to convince the police to take their concerns more seriously.

Paige, meanwhile, was going to talk to her father-in-law at his funeral home to see if there was any way he could delay the funeral.

Arden was going to go to the local library to try to track down any family or friends Ivy might have confided in before she disappeared. Savannah had suggested talking to Julie since she and Ivy had known each other and had been friends until the girl's disappearance but Arden decided against it. If Duncan Thorpe was a murderer, the last thing she wanted to do was confide in his niece. She figured she could talk to Julie later. Right now, she just wanted to gather as much background information on Ivy Kent as she could before interviewing any potential suspects or their relatives.

Annabel Allen

She walked around the library gathering local history books, high school yearbooks, old phone books and a couple of reference books which she then placed on a long desk at the back of the library, far away from other patrons.

She started with the high school books, searching for anyone with the last name Kent. She went through ten before giving up and reaching for the phone books. She wasn't sure where Ivy was from, but if the high school yearbooks were anything to go by, it was becoming clear she hadn't grown up in Cloverleaf Cove.

With a sigh, she selected a ten year old phone book from the pile in front of her and flipped it open. She had just turned to the Ks when she heard a man's deep throated laugh. She glanced behind her shoulder, surprised to find Max standing nearby.

"I know this is a small town," he said, "but we seem to be tripping over each other."

She closed the phone book and pushed it to the side as he joined her at the table.

He glanced at the telephone books stacked by her with a bemused smile. "How's the plot in those things?"

She grinned. "Oh, they're a regular page turner."

His brow furrowed as he examined the stack of books next to the phone books. "Detective Investigation Techniques," he said reading one of the titles out loud. "Old phone books and crime investigation books." He looked at her in interest. "Kind of an odd combination."

She turned the books so the spines were facing away from him. "Just a hobby of mine," she said as she fussed with lining the spine edges up with one another.

He arched an eyebrow. "Right. This wouldn't be because you think Bruce was murdered?"

Arden's mouth fell open. "How do you know that?"

"I ran into Paige an hour ago. She told me that she was investigating Bruce's murder and the murder of some girl named Ivy Kent."

Arden blew out her breath. "So much for secrecy."

"She's scared."

"So am I."

He studied her face. "You don't look scared."

"Really? And just how do I look?"

"Excited." He paused a beat before reaching for the phone book. "Who are you looking for in here?"

She hesitated for a moment. "Well, I guess the cat's out of the bag. If you must know, I'm looking for Ivy's relatives."

He gave her a look. "I see." He laid the phone book to the side. "Well, you're not going to find any of her relatives in here."

"How do you know?"

"Because I just came from the sheriff's office. After I spoke to Paige, I decided to see what the sheriff could tell me about Ivy Kent."

Her eyes widened in excitement. "And?"

"She's got a warrant out for her arrest."

"I already knew that."

"She also has no family in town or anywhere else for that matter. She was orphaned in California when she was eight years old. Lived there most of her life, bouncing from foster home to foster home until she landed in jail."

"Why was she in jail?"

"She shoplifted from a couple of stores. Stole a car once. Has a list of sundry crimes a mile long. She served her time, and then dropped off the face of Earth for a few years before showing up in Cloverleaf Cove. She was here less than six months before disappearing with Gladys Oakley's jewelry and cash. The sheriff is convinced she's back in California somewhere. There is absolutely no reason to suspect that she met with foul play here."

"But Bruce—"

"Liked to make up stories. I wouldn't believe anything he said."

"Really? Then why did you go to the police station this morning?"

The corners of his lips turned up. He tried to offer up a defense but just chuckled instead. "I was curious. It's in my nature to be curious."

"Well, me too. Did Paige tell you about the oleander plant in my yard? I think someone grabbed one of the blooms the other night and used that to poison Bruce. Oh, and by the way, you should keep Lucky away from there until Julie has a chance to dig it up."

"How many people knew you had that growing in your yard?"

She stacked the books together and set them on a nearby book cart. "Well, the prowler traipsing through my yard knew. He or she dropped an oleander bloom on my porch."

"It was storming hard that night. The wind probably blew it on your porch." He lightly touched her arm sending tingles racing up and down her arm. "Listen to me, it is not a good idea to go chasing a killer, especially one who might live a few doors away from you and has no problem knocking off his neighbors whenever he chooses. Boredom is no excuse for rushing into danger."

"I'm not bored. I'm worried. What if the killer decides to kill anyone who suspects that Ivy was murdered?"

"Well, he or she is going to be very busy. They'll have to start with everyone you and Paige have talked to this morning."

Arden felt sick. "Oh, that's not funny."

"Who else have you and Paige told your theories to?"

Arden bit her lip. She knew Max couldn't possibly be the killer since he was with her when the killer was traipsing around her backyard, but there was no reason bringing Savannah up if she didn't have to. "Hardly anyone," she muttered before adding, "Paige's not even a hundred percent convinced." He looked at her doubtfully, causing her to add, "You can't blame me for being secretive. Who knows who's next?" With that, she turned heel and walked out of the library before he could question her further. She made it as far as the steps before he caught up to her.

"Look, I don't think there's a killer living on our block," he said. "I think Bruce was probably playing one of his little jokes on..." His voice trailed off as his gaze swept over her shoulder. "Have you seen Wendy lately?"

"Not since the party. Why?"

His lips curled up. "Take a look behind you."

Arden turned around and froze, her eyes widening in shock as a newly transformed Wendy came strutting down the sidewalk in a short dress, six-inch heels and a dozen or so shopping bags dangling from her wrists. She looked stunning and not the slightest bit devastated or distressed by her grandfather's passing.

Max's voice echoed her thoughts. "She's taking her grandfather's death well," he remarked softly as the woman drew closer.

Before Wendy had a chance to pass by, Arden stepped in front of her blocking her way. "Hello, Wendy, how are you?"

Wendy blinked as if only then recognizing her. "Oh hello," she said before going through the normal social niceties one does when meeting an acquaintance on the street. "I'm fine, thank you. How are you?"

"Quite well. I tried to drop by to pay my respects yesterday but I seemed to have missed you."

"I was out. There was just so much to do."

"I'm sorry about your grandfather, Wendy," Max said gently. "When is his funeral?"

Wendy's gaze turned to Max then. Her expression changed from one of bored indifference to sex kitten in a matter of seconds. She lightly fingered the colorful butterfly pendant at her throat as she smiled up at him. "There's not going to be a funeral."

"No funeral?" Arden's eyebrows rose in surprise. "That's rather unusual."

"Granddad hated funerals. He never went to anyone else's so why should anyone go to his."

Arden wasn't sure what to say to that so she didn't say anything. It seemed strange not to have some kind of sendoff for the man. If not for him, then for his loved ones. Although at the moment, she had to wonder whether his granddaughter did in fact love him. As soon as the thought came and went, Arden mentally chided herself. Everyone grieves in their own way. Who's to say what Wendy was feeling at the moment.

Wendy tilted her face to the clear blue sky. "It's such a pretty day out. I think I might go to the beach this afternoon."

Arden glanced at Max. She could tell from the way he was looking at Wendy that his suspicions were raised. The next words out of his mouth confirmed it. "Was your granddad feeling ill the night he died?"

Wendy shrugged. "No more than usual."

"Had he been complaining about chest pains?" he asked.

A smile tugged at Wendy's mouth. "Again, no more than usual."

"Did he say anything about the food? The taste? The smell?"

"Not that I recall, but I didn't spend much time with him that night. He was in a bad mood and I told him I wasn't going to put up with it." She tilted her head to the side. "Why do you ask?"

Max hesitated for a moment. "Well, his death came as such of a shock."

"To you maybe, but not to me." She lifted her bags up. "Well, I really must be going. It was nice to see you two. Goodbye."

"Goodbye," Max and Arden said in unison as they watched her saunter away.

"Still think I'm crazy?" Arden asked softly as Wendy walked away.

"I never said you were crazy, but just because Wendy is a bit odd doesn't mean she poisoned her grandfather or killed Ivy Kent."

"No, but she is acting suspicious," she said over the sound of her cell phone ringing. She reached into her purse and pulled out her cell phone.

"Have I got news," Paige said as soon as Arden answered her phone. "I just spoke to my father-in-law. Wendy doesn't want a funeral."

"I know. We just ran into her. Have you seen her?"

"No, but he filled me in on her new look. Did she tell you that Bruce is going to be cremated first thing Monday morning? Wendy really wanted it sooner—*as soon as possible* she said—but Dad couldn't do it before then."

Glancing at Max, Arden repeated what Paige just said. "Now why would Wendy be pushing for her grandfather to be cremated as soon as possible?"

"Wendy told Dad that it's what her grandpa wanted. Oh, and guess what? As soon as Duncan showed up, he held her hand the whole entire time. Never left her side."

It wasn't Wendy and Duncan's romance that interested Arden at the moment. "If they cremate Bruce we can forget about them finding any evidence of poison."

"Let's hope Savannah can pull some strings and buy us some time," Paige said. "Look I've got to go. I'm showing the pink cottage to a couple from Maine in ten minutes. Wish me luck. I'll meet you back at your place in an hour and you can tell me what you've found out about Ivy."

"Good luck and that should be a short conversation. I think I'm going to need to talk to the Oakleys. Can you get me their number?"

"I'll text it to you. See you soon," Paige said before hanging up.

Max crossed his arms. "Well, what are we going to do next, Sherlock?"

"That's very funny. Are you willing to admit we might be on to something?"

He hesitated for a moment before he reluctantly said, "I'm not entirely convinced Bruce was murdered but I'm willing to keep an open mind."

"Good, in that case, you can help me interview the Oakleys after lunch. Do you like chicken salad sandwiches?"

His eyebrows rose and a twinkle leapt to his eye. "Is this your way of inviting me out for lunch?"

She blushed slightly. "I didn't—"

He slipped an arm around her back and steered her toward the parking lot. "Well, in that case, I'd love to *interview*   the   Oakleys."

Chapter 10

After a quick lunch in Arden's sunroom, she nervously dialed the Oakley's phone number. She wasn't sure why she was nervous but she had a feeling it was because Max was there watching her. For some silly reason, she felt like she was on a job interview. The pressure to ask the right questions and get as much information as possible weighed down on her. What if the Oakleys weren't willing to talk to her? She needed their cooperation if she was going to find out anything more about Ivy. She twisted her fingers together as she waited breathlessly for the couple to answer.

She noted that Max didn't seem ruffled in the slightest. He calmly studied the plans for the backyard lying on the round glass table between them while she drummed her fingers against the table. He glanced from the plans to Julie who was in the process of digging up the oleander bush and smiled in amusement. "If he was poisoned, you're getting rid of the murder weapon."

"If the police wanted it, they could have come and gotten it themselves. Not to mention, if that bush is the killer's favorite weapon, I want it off my property. Don't worry though, Julie is going to pot it and take it home with her and Sava—" Not wanting him to know of Savannah's involvement in their investigation, she stumbled over her name and instead said, "Paige took pictures of it and I saved a couple of blooms."

Clover, finished with her lunch, came over and rubbed herself against Max's ankles. The corners of his lips turned up as he reached down and picked her up. "*Sava-Paige,* huh? Have I met her?"

Arden shushed him as a woman's voice came on the line. Switching the phone to speaker, she laid it down in the center of the glass tabletop.

Once she introduced herself and explained why she was calling, it didn't take long for Gladys Oakley to begin talking, and to Arden's relief, she seemed more than happy to talk about Ivy Kent.

"Hiring Ivy Kent was the worst decision I ever made," Gladys Oakley said. "Wendy warned me not too trust her but I had broken my arm that summer and I needed some help around the house. Plus, I felt sorry for Ivy."

"Why was that?" Arden asked.

"Honey, I feel sorry for anyone that had to live in that house next door. She had worked for Wendy for less than a month before coming to work for us, and frankly, I'm surprised she lasted that long."

"I could imagine Bruce would be rather difficult to live with," Max remarked.

"Oh, I could too, but funny thing is Ivy actually liked the old coot. They were as thick as thieves. You should have heard them talking to one another upstairs from the balcony railings."

Arden glanced out the window just as Duncan strode into her backyard as if he owned it and approached his niece. His loud irate voice carried through the open French doors.

"Ivy liked that hateful old man," Gladys said. "It was Wendy that she hated with a passion."

Max turned his attention from the window back to the phone. "Why was that?"

"She was cruel to her. I could hear her screaming at the girl day and night."

Arden's brow furrowed. She couldn't imagine Wendy Grayson caring about anything enough to raise her voice above a placid whisper. "What was she screaming about?"

"Lots of things. Ivy wasn't that much of a housekeeper but that wasn't any reason to scream at the girl like she did. But that's just Wendy's way, I guess. She used to yell at her husband too. I blame Bruce for that though. As soon as he moved in, he started pushing them apart. It's not right to do that to a married couple. Of course, his affair only made things worse."

"Whose affair?" Max asked.

"Todd's," she answered. "I heard through the grapevine that he had been meeting with some woman in a motel outside of town that summer."

"Do you know who he was having an affair with?" Arden asked.

"Not really. You know how rumors go. Who knows what the truth is. I just know he was a good neighbor. Not like Wendy and her grandfather. Couldn't count on those two for anything."

"How did Wendy meet Ivy?" Max asked.

"Through a temp agency. Wendy needed some help around the house. Taking care of her grandfather was a full time job so she hired Ivy from some agency outside of town. A few weeks later, I found Ivy walking down the street with tears streaming from her eyes. She said that Wendy was being so mean to her that she quit. I felt so sorry for her I hired her on the spot. If I had known what she was like I would have let her keep walking. But you don't know people really until they're living in your house with you. She seemed liked such a sweet girl too. It didn't take long to realize my mistake."

"What did Ivy do?" Arden asked.

"She slept all day. Was up all hours of the night. She couldn't clean worth a darn. Then things began going missing. That should have tipped me off, but I thought it was my husband moving things around and forgetting where he put them. Wendy tried to warn me but I didn't believe her."

Max scratched underneath Clover's chin eliciting a deep-throated purr. "Warn you about what?"

"That Ivy was a thief. Wendy accused the girl of stealing some jewelry of hers and told me she'd rob me blind if I wasn't careful. I wasn't too pleased with Ivy's work at the time, but I figured Wendy was just trying to get her into trouble. Wendy can be rather vindictive at times. She wasn't too pleased when I hired Ivy and started causing trouble soon after. I'd watch her if I were you. She acts sweet but deep down she's not. Oh, by the way, is Emma still living over there?"

"Yes," Arden said idly as she watched Duncan and Julie in the backyard. From the amount of hand waving and gesturing, he was doing, he didn't seem too happy with his niece or about what she was doing in the backyard.

"I hope she doesn't throw Emma out on the street now that Bruce is dead. Poor Emma doesn't have any family and is all alone now that her husband's dead. She's only got a little social security to live on and that's it. If she loses this job, I'm not sure what she'll do. She was on the verge of being homeless when Todd hired her to take care of Bruce."

Arden bit her lip, her heart going out toward the older lady.

"Please make sure to give Emma my best."

"I will," Arden said vowing to check up on Emma to make sure she was all right. "Ivy lived with you for five months. Why do you think she stole from you?"

"You know what they say; when the cat's away the mice will play. My husband and I were celebrating our fiftieth wedding anniversary on a cruise with our whole family when Ivy decided to throw a party. We had specifically told her no parties but she went and did it anyway. You should have seen what she had done to my house. I couldn't believe my eyes when I got back home. I had always kept it so neat and clean." Her voice turned mournful as she began listing the damage to her home. "There were beer bottles, streamers and confetti everywhere. They had tracked mud all through the house. One of the panes in the French door was cracked. A couple of my prized rose bushes had been trampled on. One had even been uprooted and thrown over the gate. My coffee table was shattered. I had to throw away the rug underneath because of all the blood."

Max swung his attention away from Bruce and Julie to the phone.

"She also took all my jewelry—"

Max set Clover down on the floor, his attention now on the phone. "You found blood?"

"Yes, I did. It completely ruined the rug. She took my grandmother's necklace. I was planning to leave that necklace for my own granddaughter and she knew that but she took it anyway. She also took my favorite vase. Oh, it was so pretty. Went perfectly with my fuchsia drapes. I've never found anything that would match those drapes as well."

Arden excitedly leapt from the table. She reached into the cabinet and pulled out a glass jar containing the piece of china she had found in her yard. She handed the jar to Max. "Gladys, was the vase white with little purple flowers?"

"Well, I thought it was more fuchsia than purple but yes. My husband used to argue with me about it because he thought they were purple too but there was too much red in those drapes to be a true purple."

Max set the jar aside. "Do you know who got hurt?" he asked turning the conversation back to the bloodstained rug.

"Oh, I have no idea. She invited over a dozen people. Emma told me that as soon as the police came they all scattered like bugs. We didn't find out about it until Emma got hold of us the next day. The first thing I did was call Ivy. I told her to pack her bags and get out."

"What did she say?" Arden asked

"She swore up and down that it was just a party with a few friends and that they turned down the music as soon as the police told her someone complained. Told me she was getting engaged and just wanted to celebrate with some friends from out of town. Tried to sweet talk me into not firing her." Gladys blew out a disgusted breath. "It worked too. I told her that as long as everything was back in order by the time we got home then," she said drawing out the word, "she wouldn't have to leave."

Arden raised her eyebrows at Max. "Who was she getting engaged too?"

"Wouldn't say. I had a feeling he was a married man. Why else keep it a secret?"

"What time did you last speak to her?" Arden asked.

"It was sometime late Sunday afternoon. Ivy said that she had spent all day cleaning and that there wasn't a speck of dust or smudge of dirt anywhere in the house. Swore to me that it was cleaner than when we left it and that she was prettying up the yard for us when we called." Gladys snorted. "You should have seen that house when I got home. It looked like a tornado hit it. She's lucky she was gone by the time I got home and saw what she had done to my house."

"Did you ever speak to her again after that?" Max asked.

"No, and I don't want to speak to her. All I want is my jewelry back. She stole a necklace my grandmother wore on her wedding day and a charm bracelet that my mother gave me for my sixteenth birthday." Her voice trembled slightly. "Those had special sentimental value to me and she knew that."

Arden glanced towards the French doors as they opened. Duncan stood at the door with an angry looking Julie standing behind him glaring at his back. He loudly cleared his throat before speaking to them in short clipped tones. "I've got to borrow Julie for a few hours on the park project. I'm on a deadline. Can't be helped. We're in a bit of a hurry."

"Is that Duncan Thorpe's voice I hear?" Gladys asked her voice brightening.

A genuine smile broke out over Duncan's face. "It sure is, Gladys. When are you all going to come back and visit with us?"

Julie mouthed a silent apology to Arden as Duncan and Gladys caught up with one another. His deadline suddenly disappeared as he spent the next five minutes describing his latest project to Gladys, only stopping when she reluctantly had to say goodbye and head to a doctor's appointment.

Duncan glanced at his watch after the call was over. "Come on, Julie. Let's get a move on."

Julie threw Arden another apologetic look before following her uncle back through the yard. Duncan took hold of the wheelbarrow while Julie collected a rake, shovel and other tools she had brought with her that day and placed them in the wheelbarrow.

Arden glanced back at Max. "Now, that was suspicious."

He shook his head. "Not really. Duncan has really fallen behind on the new park. I hear the Mayor is after his head."

"I'm not talking about that. I'm talking about the business with the blood and the broken furniture."

"Oh that," he said with a small smile. "It sounded like a wild party."

"It sounded like someone was seriously hurt." She tapped a fingernail against the side of the jar. "I found this buried in the yard and look at the strand of blonde hair. I bet it's Ivy's. What if someone hit her over the head with the vase and that's what killed her?"

"We still don't know if Ivy was murdered." Max frowned as he held up the jar. "If she—" The doorbell rang cutting off his response.

"That's probably Paige," Arden said as she excused herself from the table.

To her surprise, it wasn't Paige but Savannah who walked through the door, mad as a hornet and ready to fight.

"She won't get away with this," Savannah said without preamble as she charged into Arden's house.

"Who won't get away with what?" Arden asked in concern.

"That woman! She thinks she's in charge. Ha!" Savannah flexed her fingers. "How dare she threaten me?"

Arden gasped. "Who? Wendy? Emma?"

"My daughter-in-law," Savannah ground out. "I very calmly and rationally explained to her that Bruce McCallum was poisoned in my home and that something needed to be done about it. Do you know what she told me?"

Arden caught Max out of the corner of his eye standing by the staircase and cringed.

He grinned. "So, I take it this is the other half of Sava-Paige?"

Sighing, Arden turned her attention back to the irate Savannah. "What did she say?"

"She told me that I sounded hysterical and threatened to call my son if I didn't drop this nonsense. This from a woman who is convinced that Rex Billing's pet goat can predict who is going to become the next Mayor."

"I've heard about that goat," Max said. "Apparently, he's correctly predicted every Mayor for the last ten years."

Savannah tilted her head back and closed her eyes. She breathed deeply in and out for a few moments before plastering a smile to her face. "I do so hope you had better luck than I did today."

There was a knock at the door and Paige stepped inside. She glanced from one to the other, with a hopeful smile on her face. "So, did I miss anything?"

The Perfect Recipe for Murder

Chapter 11

It was late in the afternoon by the time Paige and Savannah made their way back to their own homes. Max left shortly after Paige arrived. Not without marching orders as it were. Before he had a chance to make his escape, Savannah had taken him by the arm and sweetly asked that he try to find Ivy. If she was alive as he insisted, then surely someone had seen her in the last five years, she reasoned.

Once he was gone, Arden shared everything she had learned that morning with her two friends. Soon a general consensus started to form. Everything seemed to point to Wendy as being the killer. As Savannah pointed out, she had motive, means and opportunity.

Despite that, Arden wasn't convinced. If Wendy had killed Bruce, wouldn't she at least pretend to be the grieving granddaughter?

Then there was Ivy. They all agreed something had happened to the girl, but without more information, they couldn't say for certain that Wendy had anything to do with her disappearance. Would she have killed the girl for stealing from her?

Before Savannah and Paige left, they all resolved to seek out anyone who might have been at the party that night five years ago.

With that goal in mind, Arden anxiously waited for Julie to reappear in her backyard. If Julie and Ivy were friends, surely she would have been there that night. With any luck, Julie would be able to give her a clue as to what happened that night and possibly the name of her fiancé.

As soon as Julie appeared in her backyard, Arden stepped outside. The young woman immediately ran to Arden, apologies tumbling off her lips, until Arden stopped her.

Arden hurried to reassure the upset girl. "It's all right, Julie, I understand."

"How can you?" Julie wailed, tears threatening to spill onto her cheeks. "I don't even understand. Uncle Duncan won't even give me a chance."

"He wanted your help today," Arden pointed out. "That's good, isn't it?"

"No," she said bitterly as she swiped a finger across her red eyes. "He just wanted me to stop working. We got to the park and he sent me to get him a sandwich."

"Oh."

"He wants me to go back to school and is doing everything he can to sabotage me."

"That's kind of harsh," Arden said gently. "I'm sure your uncle has your best interests in mind."

Turning away, Julie mumbled something under her breath.

Deciding it was best to change the subject, Arden said, "Anyway, I'm glad you've come back. I've been wanting to talk to you. Why don't you come inside? I just made a pitcher of pink lemonade."

Julie looked at her in panic as she stepped onto the porch. "You're not going to fire me, are you?"

"No, of course not." She wrapped an arm around the girl's shoulders and led her into the kitchen. "To tell you the truth, I'm really curious about my new house and I'm hoping you can help me." She closed the door. "I'm trying to get an idea of the people who lived here."

Julie nodded to herself as she sat down at the kitchen table. "Ah, so that's why you were talking to Mrs. Oakley. I overheard her saying something about Ivy." A reluctant smile tugged at her lips. "I bet she gave you an earful about her."

Arden smiled as she poured Julie a glass of pink lemonade. She had wondered how she was tactfully going to turn the conversation back to Ivy and it looked like it was going to be easier than she thought it was going to be. "As a matter of fact, she did. She seemed to have…" She hesitated, trying to come up with a fitting description of Gladys Oakley's thoughts about Ivy.

"Strong opinions?" Julie offered as she took the glass of lemonade.

"Yes, very strong," Arden added ruefully. "She said that Ivy threw an engagement party for herself before she disappeared. Were you there?"

"Oh, I wouldn't have missed it." Julie grinned. "I heard there was going to be free food and I shot across the street like a bolt."

Arden laughed as she passed the package of cookies Julie was eyeing to the young woman. "What was Ivy's fiancé like?"

Julie's eye shifted to the table. "Dunno," she said drawing the word out as she took a cookie.

"Wasn't he there?"

She shook her head. "He was a no show," she said before biting into the cookie. "He might have shown up after I left though. I was only there for ten minutes."

"Why?"

Julie rolled her eyes. "My uncle found out I was there and made me go home."

"Why didn't he want you there?"

She reached for another cookie. "I had a six hour drive back to college the next morning and he said he wanted me to get a good night sleep." She shrugged. "It's just as well, Wendy called the police on them an hour later and had it shut down."

"I take the party got out of hand."

Julie grinned. "Ivy definitely knew how to throw a party back then, but that's not why Wendy called the police. Wendy only did it because she hated Ivy, but then I can hardly blame her."

Arden reached for her empty glass. "Why is that?"

Julie hesitated for a moment, but then as if sharing a juicy piece of gossip leaned forward. "I guess it doesn't matter now that they're divorced but Ivy was sleeping with Wendy's husband, Todd."

Arden raised an eyebrow. "So, Ivy and Todd Grayson were having an affair. Are you sure Wendy knew?"

"No doubt about it. Ivy told me that Wendy caught them together and that's why she threw Ivy out on her can."

"Gladys told me that Ivy quit."

"Nah, that's just what Ivy wanted people to believe. She liked people to feel sorry for her. She knew Wendy wouldn't say anything—too embarrassed—so she said whatever she had to in order to make herself look good. I kind of felt sorry for Wendy. Ivy should never have tried to seduce her husband away from her. She didn't even like Todd. It was all just a game to Ivy but Wendy really loved the creep."

Lost in thought, Arden drummed her fingers against the table. It appeared Wendy did have motive for killing Ivy. Would she really kill her own grandfather though? "What was Wendy's relationship with her grandfather like?"

Julie dusted crumbs off her t-shirt, and then shrugged. "I dunno. Not very good, I'd guess."

"Why do you say that?"

Julie shrugged again. "He was really mean to her. Always telling her what to do. Where to go. Uncle Duncan called him a control freak."

"What do you think about your uncle dating Wendy?"

There was a moment of hesitation before Julie answered, "Don't tell my uncle but I'm not too thrilled. He has the worst taste in women I've ever seen. I think she's as nutty as her grandpa but Uncle Duncan says he's in love." She looked sadly at the table. "I don't think she loves him," she confessed softly, "and I don't think she likes me much either. She's always trying to get rid of me." She blew out her breath. "I guess I don't much care for her but . . . what can you do. Uncle Duncan's in love."

"Do you think she's dangerous?"

"Wendy?" Julie blinked in confusion. "I don't think she'd hurt Uncle Duncan. Not physically at least. He's way bigger than she is. I'm just afraid she'll change him." She made a face. "Wendy's always nitpicking. She doesn't like the clothes he wears, his cowboy boots, the way he wears his hair, his taste in music. I'm telling you she's not that much different from her grandpa. She's a serious control freak." She wrinkled her nose. "She thinks she's better than us too. I wish he'd find someone else--" She suddenly looked at Arden with renewed interest.

"Are you seeing anyone? You know my uncle's a great guy. I bet you two would really hit it off."

"Oh yeah," Arden said with an uncomfortable chuckle, "um, I would but . . ." she trailed off, her gaze unintentionally traveling to the blue house next door.

Following her gaze, Julie's eyes widened. She grinned. "Oh. I see. Max's really hot, isn't he?"

Arden cleared her throat, and then promptly changed the subject. "Anyway, when was the last time you saw Ivy?"

"The next morning. I stopped by to tell her goodbye before I headed back to school."

"Were you surprised when you heard she left with the Oakley's things?"

She sighed. "I hate talking badly about Ivy. She was a friend but to be honest, no, I wasn't that surprised, not after I caught her in my uncle's bedroom going through his stuff."

Arden frowned. "Did she say what she was doing in there?"

"No, she made some excuse. I figured she was looking for money. She had been complaining about the price of plane tickets for weeks."

"Oh? Was she going somewhere?"

"Yeah, I think she knew her days around here were numbered."

Arden started to take a sip and paused. "What makes you think that?"

"It just seemed like everyone was angry with her for one reason or another." There was a moment of silence, then Julie added, "You know that day I went over to say goodbye? I saw something really strange."

Arden sat up straighter. "What?"

"Ivy was acting weird and I noticed that she kept covering her face with her hair or her hand. She accidentally forgot for a moment to do it and I saw this giant red welt along her cheek." Julie grimaced. "I think someone smacked her around and hard. I asked what had happened but she wouldn't say. Her eyes were red too. Like she had been crying and she seemed . . . scared. I don't know why but I got the feeling she was about to run." She turned her attention to the window. "Wherever she is, I hope she's okay."

"Me too," Arden said softly.

Julie finished her glass with one gulp and set it aside. "Oh hey, I've got some good news at least. Wendy has a really pretty birdbath in her garage that she absolutely hates."

Arden's brow furrowed. "Why does she have a birdbath in her garage?"

"Well, it used to be in her backyard but she had Uncle Duncan move it last month so she could put in a vegetable garden." She held up her hands. "Don't ask me why, I have no idea. All she would say was that she was sick of looking at the thing. It's ugly too. The garden not the birdbath," she quickly explained. "Uncle Duncan offered to put in something better but she wanted to do it herself. Anyway, I asked her if I could have the birdbath and she said yes. It won't cost you a thing." She reached into her pocket and pulled out her phone. She swiped through her pictures until one of a charming fluted birdbath appeared. "I think this would be perfect for your garden. If you like it, I can put it in tomorrow night." She held out the phone. "So, what do you think?"

"I think it's perfect." Arden glanced across the table towards the purple house just visible above the hedge. A shiver went through her. "Just perfect."

Chapter 12

The next morning, Arden stepped out of the church and into the bright morning sun humming to herself as she walked down the sidewalk towards the parking lot. She started to reach into her purse for her car keys, but stopped when she noticed Savannah standing in the parking lot talking to a police officer.

Arden probably wouldn't have thought anything about it if it weren't for the suspicious way they were acting. They stood next to Savannah's car, each looking over their shoulders as they huddled close together. Arden's eyes widened as the officer slipped a manila envelope to Savannah who quickly stuffed it into her purse.

Paige and her family slowed to a stop next to Arden. Shielding her eyes from the sun, she stared out across the parking lot with a frown on her face. "I wonder what that's about."

"I don't know," Arden said, biting her lip. "Do you think Savannah is in some kind of trouble?"

"What?" Paige followed Arden's gaze. "Not her. *Her*," she said pointing to a figure standing in the graveyard beyond the rows of cars lined up along the grassy bank in the distance.

Wendy, draped head to toe in black, stood alone among the tombstones staring up at a giant oak tree.

"I'm surprised Duncan isn't with her," Arden said.

Paige shook her head. "He goes to a different church."

The officer let out a large belly laugh earning a look of disgust. Planting one hand on her hip, she gave the officer a withering look until the laughter stopped.

Paige lightly touched her husband's arm. "Sweetie, I think I'm going to stick around here for a little bit. Arden can give me a ride back home."

"Are you sure?" Patrick asked.

"I'm sure." Standing on her tiptoes, she gave her husband a kiss on the cheek before sending him off with their daughter. By the time they were done saying goodbye, Savannah was skipping across the parking lot towards them, the enveloped clutched to her chest.

"I've got it," Savannah whispered as soon as she reached their side.

Paige softly clapped her hands together. "Yay!"

Arden glanced from Paige to Savannah. "Got what? What are you talking about?"

Spotting a group of people coming toward them, Savannah inclined her head to the side then led the two to a bench in the graveyard. Once seated, she glanced around to make sure they were alone, before slipping the envelope out of her purse and handing it to Arden who was sitting in the middle. "There are some perks to being the former mayor."

Arden slipped the papers out of the envelope and gasped. "The Oakley investigation."

"Pictures, interviews, the whole shebang." Savannah glanced over her shoulder. "I hope that woman doesn't catch us."

"Wendy?" Arden asked glancing toward the tree to see if Wendy was still around.

"No, my daughter-in-law. If she finds out Spencer slipped this to me she will have his badge." She smiled, clearly pleased with herself. "It's nice to know I still have some influence left in this town."

"Did you tell the police what we suspect?" Arden asked. "Does this mean they finally believe us?"

Savannah blew out her breath in annoyance. "For some reason, they refuse to believe that an 89 year old man, who liked to tell tall tales and who had a list of aliments a mile long and didn't have very much longer to live, might have been poisoned because someone, may have possibly, overheard him telling you that a girl, who no one thinks is dead, was murdered."

"Well, when you put it like that . . ." Paige said ruefully.

Arden frowned. "What do you mean he didn't have long to live? My great-grandmother lived to be ninety-nine and she had a host of health problems too."

"I bet they weren't anything like Bruce's problems," Paige said. "Patrick was his doctor. He told me that Bruce had been living on borrowed time for quite a while."

Savannah scowled. "The police won't even entertain the idea that he might have been murdered. They're convinced he had a heart attack."

"But what about the person in my yard?" Arden sputtered. "The oleander? The fact that Wendy is rushing to cremate him and that no one has seen Ivy Kent since she supposedly left town?"

Savannah rolled her eyes. "Spencer said that there could be a perfectly logical explanation for all of it and that we should turn off the soaps and stop creating drama where there isn't any. Then he laughed at me when I insisted the old man was murdered." She pursed her lips together. "If it weren't for the fact that I was in a church parking lot when he said that, you'd be visiting me in jail for assaulting a cop right now." She lifted her eyes up to the heavens and smiled wistfully. "I could just imagine my daughter-in-law's face if she found out I had been arrested right before her big election." She glanced back towards the parking lot. "I wonder if Spencer is still around."

Before Savannah could give into any dark impulses she might have, Arden opened the file and said, "Well, hopefully we'll find something in here that will help us."

"You know," Savannah said thoughtfully, "there is another option we haven't considered."

"What?" Arden asked.

"Well, I was just thinking that there is one of us," Savannah said giving Paige a meaningful look, "that has access to a potential piece of evidence that would definitely prove whether Bruce was poisoned or not."

Paige's brow furrowed in confusion. "What are you talking about?"

"Bruce's body is sitting in your father-in-law's morgue," Savannah pointed out.

Arden's mouth dropped open as Savannah added, "What if Patrick or his dad just saved a little piece of Bruce's stomach?" She held up her hands as Arden eyes widened and Paige's mouth moved in wordless shock and horror. "Now don't say no right off the bat. Just think, we could send that piece to the lab then we'd have proof whether old Bruce was murdered or not. I remember filming an episode where my character broke into a funeral home one night and bribed Morty the Mortician to do an impromptu autopsy on some guy."

"Eww," Paige said.

Savannah smiled happily in remembrance. "We found a great clue and we solved the case."

"It was the county morgue," Arden pointed out. "And the victim was Miss Fowler the chemistry teacher and the mortician's name was Henry. The autopsy never happened because the killer found out what Sunny was up to and tried to kill her at the morgue. While Clay was fighting him, Sunny found a ticket stub which proved that the killer was the principal." At Savannah and Paige's look, Arden said a bit defensively, "What? I have a good memory."

Savannah thought about it for a moment, and then shook her head. "Still, it's a great idea." She glanced at Paige. "Someone here should try it."

"Have you lost your ever-loving mind?" Paige asked when she finally found her voice. "I'm not going to ask my father-in-law to do that. He could get into a lot of trouble. Besides, he believes Bruce died of old age too." Paige's lips pursed together in a thin line. "He and Patrick were laughing about our little theories last night. What I wouldn't give to prove them wrong." She glanced over Arden's shoulder. "What does the police report say?"

Arden turned her attention back to the police report. There wasn't much about Ivy and her relationship with their neighbors in the file, but what was there was very telling.

"A few days after Ivy disappeared," Arden read, "the police found her car abandoned in a bus station three hours from here."

Paige tucked her hair behind her ears as she read over Arden's shoulder. "And it says that the last person that saw Ivy the day she disappeared was Bruce. Maybe he did know something after all." She tapped a pink fingernail against the paper in Arden's hand. "Look at this. He watched her cleaning up the yard and house from eleven to two o'clock Sunday. He talked to her for a few minutes, and then he went inside and took a nap. By the time he woke up a couple of hours later, she was gone and the Oakley's house was dark."

Arden flipped through the pages, stopping at a picture of the smashed coffee table. "Cleaning up? This doesn't look like she cleaned up anything."

Savannah pointed to the corner of the picture. "Look at that thing there in the corner of the room. Doesn't that look like an empty trash bag? What if she cleaned up like Bruce said but the killer came back and trashed the place again?"

"Why?" Paige asked. "What would be the point of trashing the Oakley's home?"

"To cover up her murder?" Arden mused. "After all, what thief goes to the trouble of cleaning the house before robbing it? The killer may have wanted to make her look as bad as possible."

"But the police knew she cleaned everything up," Paige said. "Bruce told them."

Savannah lightly snorted. "They were probably well aware of Bruce's reputation and ignored his statement."

Paige sighed as she turned her attention back to the report. "Did anyone else see her that day?"

Arden flipped back to the witness statements. "Julie told the police that she saw her that morning before she left for college. She told me the same thing yesterday after you all left. Said she saw a giant welt on Ivy's face as if someone had hit her." She frowned down at Julie's statement. "That's not in her statement. I wonder why she didn't tell the police about that."

"Maybe she forgot," Paige said.

Arden bit her lip. "Or maybe she was protecting someone."

Paige suddenly stood. "Wendy left. I'm going to go over and see what was so special about that tree. Be right back."

While Paige skipped through the graveyard, Arden and Savannah continued pouring over Julie's statement. "Look at this," Arden said, "Julie told the police that Ivy stole her grandma's wedding ring."

"When?" Savannah asked.

"A few days before Ivy disappeared. She wanted to call the police right then but her uncle told her that he'd handle it himself."

"That sounds ominous."

Arden flipped back through the police report. "Duncan didn't make a statement about the theft. Doesn't look like they even spoke to him."

Paige hurried back. "Did I miss anything?"

"Just that Ivy stole Julie's grandmother's wedding ring," Savannah said, "and Duncan was kind enough not to report her."

"I don't buy that for a second," Paige said. "One of his employees stole twenty dollars from him and he called the cops on the guy." She glanced at Savannah. "Who is Diana McCallum?"

"Bruce's wife. She died about ten years ago. Why?"

"Her grave is by that tree," Paige said. "She's underneath one of those husband and wife stones, which makes it seem like at some point Bruce planned on being buried next to his wife. Seems kind of strange that they're going to cremate Bruce and not bury him with his wife." She glanced down at Wendy's police statement. "Oooh, it appears Wendy's ruby ring went missing while Ivy was working for her. She couldn't prove that Ivy was the one who took it but she suspected she had and fired her."

Arden pursed her lips together. "That wasn't the reason she fired Ivy."

"You know something we don't?" Savannah asked.

Arden raised her eyebrows. "Let's just say Wendy discovered Ivy taking better care of her husband than her grandfather."

Paige gasped. "That's our motive then. Wendy killed Ivy because she was sleeping with Wendy's husband and then she killed her own grandfather because he knew about the murder."

"Wendy wouldn't know an oleander bush from a rose bush," Savannah said. "That might be an exaggeration but not by much. As for Ivy, she wasn't the first girl that Wendy caught sleeping with her husband and they're all still alive as far as I know. No, I don't think we can immediately assume Wendy killed her grandfather. It seems to me that it would be less risky to kill him at home. A pillow over the face. A push down a flight of stairs."

Paige cringed. "Savannah!"

Savannah nodded to herself. "I think the killer took a risk because he or she had no other opportunity to get to him. At least not quickly enough before he blabbed any more than he already had. If you ask me, Duncan is just as likely a killer as Wendy."

"Duncan?" Paige frowned. "But why would he kill Ivy?"

"Because Ivy was a jewel thief." Savannah tapped a fingernail against the police report. "She stole Julie's grandmother's wedding ring, and then when he found out about it, he decided not to call the police. He told Julie that he'd handle it. Perhaps, he confronted Ivy about the ring, got angry and killed her. Then he overheard Bruce talking about the murder and realized he had to kill him too."

Something Max said the night of the party came back to Arden just then and she chuckled. "Do you remember the stories Bruce used to tell? According to Max, Bruce accused Duncan of being the jewel thief, not Ivy."

Savannah snorted. "Crazy old man. He used to tell everyone that my father was a mad scientist who performed freakish experiments in our cellar. I offered to take him down there once but he wouldn't go."

Arden flipped through the insurance pictures of Gladys Oakley's missing jewelry until a familiar looking butterfly pendant caught her eye. "This looks familiar. Wendy was wearing it yesterday morning," Arden added with a meaningful look.

Savannah took the report and held it up closer to her eyes. "Are you sure?"

"I'm sure," Arden said. "The question is where did she get it? According to this report, Ivy was the one who stole it."

"See!" Paige crowed. "I was right. That proves Wendy is the killer. She killed Ivy and then took a little memento home with her."

"I think you might be right," Arden said, a thrill of excitement racing through her. "Wendy has motive, means and opportunity."

"But how are we going to prove it?" Savannah asked. "Bruce is scheduled to be cremated tomorrow and we're running out of time."

Arden stuffed the report back into the envelope and handed it to Savannah. "You know, I think we've been derelict in our Christian duties."

"How so?" Paige asked.

Arden rose to her feet. "I think it's high time we visit the bereaved."

Chapter 13

Wendy opened the door with a look of surprise on her face as Arden, Paige and Savannah presented three platters of food.

"Oh hello," Wendy said, reluctantly stepping back to allow the other three women to enter.

The sound of heavy feet stomping down the stairs caught their attention and they looked up just as Emma came into view on the staircase landing. With a suitcase in each hand, she squared her shoulders and slowly descended the staircase. She smiled sadly at the women, saying nothing as she passed by.

Emma's stricken expression tugged at Arden's heartstrings. "Emma," she said with a concerned look, "where are you going?"

Emma paused in the doorway for a moment. She opened her mouth to say something, but then decided against it and simply shook her head.

Wendy hurriedly ushered the older woman out the door. "Goodbye, Emma, and thank you for being so understanding."

Emma's chin lifted slightly. She nodded quietly before walking down the porch stairs with her head held high.

Savannah tipped her head to the side, regarding Wendy with an amused smile as the other woman closed the door. "I hope we didn't come at a bad time."

Politeness forced Wendy into immediate denial. "No, of course not. I'm happy to see you."

A piece of paper lay on the dark wooden console table near the door. Arden glanced down surprised to see what appeared to be a job announcement for a housekeeper. Wendy certainly didn't let grass grow under her feet. She would have thought Wendy would have waited until Bruce was cremated at least before asking Emma to leave. She exchanged a look with Paige and Savannah before asking with forced innocence, "Is Emma going on vacation?"

There was a moment's pause, and then Wendy said, "No, since Grandpa is no longer with us, I just felt that there really isn't any point for Emma to stay on."

"Where is she going to go?" Savannah asked. "I don't think she has any family to speak of."

Clearly unconcerned by such matters, Wendy simply shrugged. "I'm sure she'll find someplace."

"Oh." Worry for the older woman spurred Arden towards the door. "You know, I've been thinking about hiring some help, perhaps Emma—"

"I would suggest hiring someone else," Wendy said, her hand still firmly on the doorknob. "Don't get me wrong. Emma is a very nice woman but I've noticed she's been having some trouble climbing ladders lately. She hasn't dusted the chandeliers in quite some time. Her eyesight's not as good as it used to be either and she's been missing spots on the windows too. She and I had a long talk and we both agreed it was time for her to retire. Honestly, I think she'll be much happier now."

An uncomfortable silence descended in the room then and was only broken when Wendy extended her hand to towards the back of the house. "I was just about to have lunch. Would you like to join me?"

"Oh, that would be lovely," Savannah said. "Thank you."

Arden glanced out the window next to the door just as Emma climbed into an old beat up sedan and drove away. Reluctantly, she turned and followed Wendy down a dark hallway and into a narrow utilitarian kitchen.

Wendy quickly ushered them onto the patio at the back of the house while she put away the dishes of food they had brought.

While Wendy mysteriously busied herself in the kitchen, turning on and off the faucet, opening and shutting doors, and rattling dishes against one another, Arden, Paige and Savannah moved to a pretty cast iron table, painted robin's egg blue, sitting at the end of the patio.

"Thank you so much for thinking of me," Wendy called out through the open window above the sink. "That was very kind of you."

"I'm sorry it's taken so long," Paige said as Wendy disappeared from view.

Wendy poked her head out of the door long enough to say, "I do hope you'll be able to make it to the service tomorrow."

Paige looked up at her in surprise as she dusted off her chair and sat down. "So, there will be a service? I thought . . ." She trailed off as Wendy stepped back into the kitchen.

Wendy's face appeared at the window again. "I decided that it wouldn't be proper not to have some kind of sendoff," she said over the sound of running water.

"Does that mean you're not cremating your grandfather?"

There was silence.

"Perhaps she didn't hear," Arden said.

Just then, Wendy stepped outside. "No, I heard," she said wrapping an apron around her waist. "We're still going through with the cremation. That's what my grandfather wanted, but I didn't see any reason not to give everyone a chance to say their goodbyes." She turned and disappeared back into the kitchen.

Arden smoothed out her dress and sat down next to Savannah. "What time will the service be?" she asked raising her voice.

"Two," came the far away response.

"That buys us a little more time," Paige whispered.

"Not by much," Savannah replied darkly. "I think we need to talk to Emma."

"Wendy didn't waste much time in getting rid of her," Paige said. "Poor Emma. I hope she has someplace to go."

Arden frowned as Wendy moved back and forth in front of the window. "Can we help?" she asked rising from her seat.

Wendy poked her head at the door. "I wouldn't hear of it. Sit please." She waved her hands in a downward motion only stopping when Arden sat down.

"We certainly don't mean for you to trouble yourself, Wendy," Savannah called out.

"No trouble," came the reply. "Won't take me more than a minute."

Paige craned her neck to get a better look inside the house. "If you just want to pop my casserole into the microwave, we could have that for lunch."

A smiling Wendy appeared at the door again. "Oh, I thought I would save that for dinner. Duncan's taking me to a concert tonight and now I'll have dinner ready for us when we get back. I've heard him rave about your tuna casserole."

Savannah dropped her voice to a whisper when Wendy disappeared from view again. "When did you serve Duncan tuna casserole?" she asked Paige.

Paige lifted her hands in a shrug. "Maybe at one of the potlucks we had last year. I don't remember." She removed the light pink sweater she was wearing and laid it on the back of her chair before making a face. "It's so hot out here."

Nodding, Arden lifted her hair off the back of her neck as the hot sun beat down on them and blew out her breath.

With nothing else to do but wait, they leaned against the hard iron backs of their chairs and looked around. The yard, by and large, wasn't much different from any of the other yards on the street. Tall box hedges enclosed the backyard on either side, leading to a slightly smaller hedge at the back.

The only difference that Arden could spot was that Wendy's back hedge was even more overgrown than Arden's and the wrought iron gate at the back was covered by some type board completely cutting off the view of the ocean. Her gaze swept from the gate to the vegetable garden in the center of the yard flanked on either side by a couple of white and pink crepe myrtles and a . . .

Arden frowned. Tilting her head to the side, she squinted her eyes, not quite sure if she was seeing what she was seeing. She pointed to the potted pink bush sitting near the dirt patch. "I think that's my oleander bush."

Before Savannah and Paige could respond, Wendy appeared at their side with a serving tray containing china in a pretty floral pattern and tall glasses filled with ice. Setting the tray on the table, she followed Arden's pointing finger. "Why yes, that's your oleander bush, or rather, it *was* your oleander bush. I hope you don't mind, but since you didn't want it anymore, I thought I would take it."

"No, I don't mind at all," Arden said. "I'm just surprised to see it here."

"Well, when Julie stopped by to inquire about my birdbath, she mentioned that you were getting rid of the oleander bush. I thought it would be a nice trade. She's going to plant it in my garden sometime today." Wendy disappeared back into the house returning a few seconds later with a platter of sandwiches cut into triangles and a pitcher of iced tea. "I hope you like mint cucumber sandwiches. I grew the cucumbers myself."

"I've been thinking about adding a vegetable garden myself," Paige said reaching for a cucumber sandwich.

Wendy poured each of them a glass of iced tea as they filled their plates with the sandwiches. "I just love fresh vegetables. I've been taking cooking classes on the weekends for a few months now. My teacher highly recommends having your very own vegetable garden."

Feeling the effects of the scorching sun beating down on her, Arden reached for the ice tea glass and took a sip. "I've been thinking about taking cooking classes."

"You should," Wendy said as she set the pitcher down and took a seat between Arden and Paige. "I've learned a lot in just a few short months."

Savannah laid a napkin in her lap. "I'm surprised you put the garden right between those two trees. It doesn't seem like your garden would get enough sun."

Wendy smiled as they began to eat. "You sound like Duncan." She tucked her hair behind her ears, showing off a pair of beautiful diamond earrings. "He complains about the garden all the time. He wants to do something grand back here." She laughed lightly. "I sometimes wonder if the only reason he is paying so much attention to me lately is because he wants my business." She waved her hand dismissively. "Oh, would you listen to me? Grandpa always said I was too negative. I can't help it though. Whenever anyone's being nice to me, I just automatically assume they have an ulterior motive." She laughed again. "Can you believe that?"

Savannah laughed with her while Arden and Paige gave a half-hearted chuckle.

"I'm so glad you all stopped by," Wendy said picking up her sandwich. "If I had known I was going to have company I would have made my grandmother's ham salad. I remember watching her make it whenever her friends came over for a visit."

"Oh no," Savannah said, waving a hand towards the tea sandwiches. "This is absolutely delicious. I'm just sorry you went to so much trouble. We should be taking care of you right now."

"Well, this is a rare treat." Wendy nibbled on her sandwich, and then set it aside. "No one ever cared to visit me before my grandfather died."

Arden felt a pang of sympathy at the loneliness in Wendy's voice. It must have been hard living here, in some ways apart from everyone else.

Savannah delicately cleared her throat while Paige fussed with the neckline of her dress. "Yes, well," Savannah said, "I apologize that we didn't come sooner."

Sensing their discomfort, Wendy rushed to reassure them. "Oh, please don't think I'm blaming you. You were always kind enough to invite me to your parties, and for that, I've been very grateful. I'm just sorry I wasn't ever able to reciprocate. My grandfather made things…difficult sometimes." She paused reflectively and said somewhat defensively. "He wasn't a bad man."

"No, of course not," Savannah said. "I rather liked Bruce."

Wendy looked doubtful. "In small doses? He used to be great fun. It's just as he got older, he became more set in his ways. He simply lost the inclination most people had not to be a jerk to their neighbors."

Shocked into laughter, they nodded in agreement and soon, to Arden's surprise, an easy companionship developed among the four women as the conversation moved to happy memories of Bruce. Now that Wendy was relaxed and laughing, Arden realized Wendy was actually quite charming and a part of her began to feel guilty for the suspicious thoughts she had been harboring against her. Perhaps she was judging the woman too quickly.

A lock of red hair fell into Wendy's eyes and she whisked it away with a brush of her hand.

Arden gestured to her hair. "I have been meaning to tell you that I really like what you've done with your hair. It's very pretty."

A bright smile appeared on Wendy's face. "Thank you. It was time for a change."

Savannah waved her hand over her sandwich, swiping at an insect that got too close to her plate. "I've noticed that you've changed quite a bit since your grandfather died. Was he very particular about how you looked?"

A bead of perspiration appeared at Wendy's temple. Chuckling, she used her napkin as a fan, stirring up the hot muggy air. "Goodness no. I don't think he ever noticed what I wore or did. The only reason I didn't dress up more often is because there was very little point. Like I said earlier, no one ever visited us and I had no hope of a social life with him around."

"Duncan didn't seem to mind the way you dressed," Paige said with a grin. "We've noticed that you and he seem to have become..." She looked heavenward as she tried to come up with the correct description. "Closer, perhaps?"

Wendy looked thoughtful. "He asked me to marry him last night."

Arden wondered if she looked as shocked as Savannah and Paige. "Congratulations!"

"I said he asked," Wendy said in amusement, "I didn't say I accepted. He reminds me a little too much of my ex-husband. But who knows, we might eventually get married. He is rather nice and I think this house could get lonely with just me here."

Paige frowned. "You wouldn't want to move into his house? He has a gourmet kitchen, a gorgeous master bath, a pool, a finished basement and seven hundred more square feet than this house." In reaction to Arden and Savannah's surprised look, she said, "It's my business to know these things."

Wendy's brow furrowed as she traced her finger over the rim of her full glass. "Why should I uproot my life?"

Paige jerked a thumb over her shoulder. "It's only next door."

"I live here. If he wants me, he can move." Wendy folded her arms across her chest. "I'll never leave here. This is my home."

Noticing Arden, Savannah and Paige's almost empty glasses of tea, Wendy leaned forward to pick up the pitcher and as she did, the butterfly pendant that had once belonged to Gladys Oakley slipped out from underneath her dress and dangled from her neck, drawing their attention to the colorful stones.

Paige gasped, drawing Wendy's attention to her and then down to the necklace. "Is there something wrong?" she asked as she refilled their glasses.

Show time, Arden thought, as she picked up her glass and took a drink. "That's a pretty necklace," she said. "It's rather unusual looking. Where did you get it?"

Setting the pitcher down, Wendy looked down at her necklace as though she wasn't sure what she was referring to. "It was my grandmother's."

"She gave it to you?" Paige asked.

"No, I found it in my grandfather's room when I was cleaning it out the other morning." Wendy caught the suspicious expressions on their face and frowned. "Why? What's wrong?"

Savannah pushed aside her plate and folded her arms on the table. "Gladys Oakley had a necklace just like that I believe. Supposedly, Ivy Kent stole it."

Wendy's eyes widened a bit. "Really? Are you sure?" At their nods, she said, "How bizarre. I wonder how it ended up in my grandfather's room." She shrugged lightly. "Perhaps Ivy gave it to my grandfather before she left. They seemed to like one another." She tipped her head forward as she reached behind her neck.

Paige's hands fluttered above her head, swiping at an insect buzzing around. "Wouldn't he have told Mrs. Oakley that Ivy had given him her necklace?"

Wendy made a face. "I doubt it. He and Gladys didn't much care for one another. Not that I could blame him. Gladys was a bit of a snob." She held up the necklace, stretching her arm towards Savannah who was sitting across from her. "I hope you don't mind returning this to Gladys. Please apologize to her for me. I would do it myself but I'm not at all sure where she moved."

Savannah picked up her purse with a nod and slipped the necklace inside. "Did Ivy often give women's jewelry to your grandfather?"

"No, but I can't imagine how it got into my house otherwise," Wendy said. "It had to have come from her."

Silence descended on the table as a subtle tension began to build.

Searching for some neutral topic of conversation, Arden held up her glass and looked at the amber liquid. "What kind of tea is this?"

"It's an herbal tea I made myself," Wendy said, her voice hardening ever so slightly. "It's an old recipe from my grandmother." Her eyes glittered as she speared each of the ladies with a menacing glance. "I crushed up some leaves from a couple of those bushes out there and made tea from them."

A feeling of horror came over Arden as her gaze zeroed in on the oleander bush and then on Wendy's untouched glass of tea.

The same thing must have occurred to Paige who suddenly choked on her drink. Quickly putting her glass down, she covered her mouth and turned to the side with a cough.

Savannah slowly swallowed with a pained expression on her face. "You don't say."

Whatever good feeling Arden had for Wendy evaporated. "You gave us oleander tea?"

Wendy raised an eyebrow. "Oleander?" She laughed. "Don't be stupid." She held up her iced tea glass with a smile. "This is lavender mint tea." A fake note of innocence crept into her voice. "You wouldn't be dumb enough to think that I would deliberately try to poison someone, would you?" Her smile grew wider. "Oh, by the way, Savannah, I ran into your daughter-in-law today at church." She held up the glass in a mock toast. "She sends you her best."

Chapter 14

"She's on to us," Paige declared angrily as they walked away from Wendy's house a few minutes later. She flung her hand back towards the house. "That was a warning for us to back off."

Savannah strode ahead of them, her hands clenching and unclenching. "That, that, that *woman* my son married obviously filled her in on what we were thinking. Oh, when I get my hands on her…"

Paige lifted her hands to her temples as she rushed to keep up with Savannah's long strides. "I can't believe we just sat there and had lunch with her. We suspected her of poisoning her grandfather and despite that, we actually sat down and had lunch with her. What were we thinking?"

"Oh honey," Savannah chided. "Wendy's not that crazy. She wasn't going to poison all three of us. She'd never get away with it."

"Still," Arden said, "Paige is right. We weren't thinking." She came to a stop at the end of the sidewalk and glanced back at the house. "We should have started somewhere else."

Savannah turned around. "What do you mean?"

"We were talking to the wrong person. If we want to find out whether Wendy could have killed Ivy, we should be speaking to someone who knew them both," she raised her eyebrows, "intimately."

A slow smile crossed Savannah's face. "Todd Grayson."

Arden nodded. "Do you know where he is?"

Paige raised her hand. "I do. I sold him a charming bungalow about thirty miles from here in Marshton." She reached into her purse and pulled out her car keys. "I could drive us over there right now."

Savannah tucked her purse under her arm. "Might as well. I love Sunday afternoon drives in the country."

Arden did too but she barely noticed the scenery as they made the trek to Todd Grayson's home over long winding roads canopied by wisteria covered trees. To pass the time, they talked about Wendy, and about whether she could have killed her grandfather. Savannah and Paige seemed convinced Wendy was the killer but Arden wasn't so sure. Wendy was definitely a cold character, but still, would she really kill her own grandfather? And if so, would she then plant the murder weapon, as it were, in her own backyard for everyone to see?

Savannah was of the opinion that Wendy was arrogant enough to do just that.

"Just what kind of woman are we dealing with?" Arden asked.

"A very dangerous one," Paige remarked.

They spent the rest of the drive in silence, only speaking when Paige pulled in front of a tiny ranch style house no bigger than Arden's garage.

Savannah raised an eyebrow at Paige as they climbed out of the car. "You call this matchbox charming?"

"He's single and Wendy took everything in the divorce." Paige tilted her chin up. "I think it's utterly charming."

The door opened then, and a handsome young man with thick dark hair and a devilish smile stepped out followed by a pair of hunting dogs.

Smiling, Paige lifted up her hand as the dogs eagerly ran towards them barking and baying as loudly as possible. "Hey Todd," she said over the sound of the enthusiastic greeting of the dogs. "I'm sorry to come unannounced, but do you have a moment to talk to us?"

Todd clapped his hands, calling the dogs to him before welcoming them inside the house. He seemed happy, if not a bit curious, to have visitors as he cleaned off the couches, doing his best to remove the dog hair.

Savannah got to the point of their visit as soon as they sat down and to no one's surprise Todd Grayson seemed only too happy to talk about his ex-wife.

"She's crazy," he said automatically and with a matter-of-fact tone of voice. "I'm sorry to hear Bruce's dead. He could be a pain but he wasn't all bad. When's the service?"

"Tomorrow," Arden answered, "at two."

His head turned towards what she assumed was the bedroom. "I'll have to press my suit," he said idly.

"Did Bruce ever talk to you about Ivy's death?" Savannah asked.

His head abruptly swung towards her. "Ivy's dead?" he asked, shock coloring his voice. "When did she die?"

Arden softened her voice. Whatever she felt about his affair, he may have cared for the girl at one time and she had no wish to cause pain to anyone. "We think she was murdered five years ago."

Stunned, Todd Grayson sat back and blinked at them. "Murdered? By who?"

"That's what we we're trying to find out," Paige said. "Do you have any idea who would have wanted to kill her?"

"Wendy," was his automatic response. "She hated Ivy."

"Because of your affair?" Savannah asked bluntly.

Todd's eyes rolled back into his head. "There was no affair." At their disbelieving looks, he added, "Okay, I cheated but it wasn't with Ivy and it wasn't until Wendy moved all my stuff into the downstairs bedroom."

Arden shook her head. "I heard that Wendy caught you and Ivy together."

He blew out a disgusted breath, clearly annoyed with having to explain himself. "Ivy was crying and I gave her a hug to comfort her." He spread out his hands. "That was the extent of our relationship. I swear."

Arden narrowed her eyes. "Ivy apparently told others that there was more to your relationship than that."

Todd snorted. "I'm not surprised."

"Why was she crying?" Paige asked.

"Because Wendy was being mean to her. She was always mean to her. She was jealous of her and didn't trust me at all. As soon as the temp agency sent Ivy to us, she was out to get the girl."

"Why didn't she just let her go?" Savannah asked.

"The old man liked Ivy and what he wanted he usually got. Wendy resented her being around and kept trying to drive her away. When that didn't work, she resorted to trying to have her arrested for theft."

Paige's eyes widened. "Arrested? Just because she didn't like her?"

"Yeah." He rested his ankle across his knee and leaned back. "She made up some bull about Ivy stealing her ruby ring. Then she tried to trick the girl into wearing it so she could prove Ivy was a thief."

Arden, Paige and Savannah exchanged a look. "How was she going to trick her?" Arden asked.

"About a week after the ring supposedly disappeared, Ivy marched over to our place with the thing in her hand. She said she found it lying on her bed with a note asking her to wear it that night during one of your parties," he said gesturing to Savannah. "She shoved it into my hand and told me to tell Wendy that the next time she left her a gift it should be diamonds."

Savannah frowned. "What did you do?"

"I put the ring back in Wendy's jewelry box." He shrugged his broad shoulders. "Never heard another word about it."

"When was the last time you saw Ivy?" Arden asked.

"At the party she threw before she left."

"You didn't see her at all the next day?"

He made a face. "It was five years ago," he complained. "I don't remember." His gaze lost focus for a moment and then he reluctantly added, "I might have seen her a few minutes."

"Do you remember what time?" Paige asked with a hopeful note in her voice.

"It had to be after two o'clock," he said with a shrug. "I used to work a few hours on the weekends. Always got home by two." His brow furrowed. "Actually, I think I did see her that day. It was right before I took Emma to the emergency room."

"Why?" Arden asked.

"She was over at the Oakleys doing something— don't really remember what—but she ended up getting stung by a wasp." He nodded suddenly. "Now I remember. Ivy brought her over to us. Emma was covered in stings and breathing funny so I ended up taking her to the emergency room. By the time Emma and I returned home, Ivy was gone but I didn't find that out until the next day."

Paige dusted a dog hair off her dress. "How did you find out she had left?"

"Duncan told me. She left him a letter saying goodbye."

Arden glanced at Savannah and Paige to see if they were as surprised as she was by that little fact. "That was nice of her. What made him so special?"

A guarded look came over Todd's eyes. "I don't know. Maybe I'm confused. It was a long time ago. All I know is that I never saw her again." He started to rise out of his chair. "Would you all like something to drink?"

Savannah scooted to the edge of the couch and speared Todd with a look. "No, no, let's go back to the letter. Why would Ivy leave Duncan a letter?"

"Ask Duncan," Todd said sitting back down with a sigh. "How should I know?"

Savannah smiled. "I don't know but somehow you do. If you didn't you wouldn't be trying so hard to backtrack right now." When he started to protest, she chuckled. "I have four boys. I can see right through you. Now, why would Ivy leave Duncan a letter?"

"I told you," he said in an annoyed voice, "it was a long time ago. I'm probably thinking of something else."

"Right now," Arden said, "we only have your word that you weren't having an affair with Ivy. If she was murdered, you're going to have to do some explaining to someone."

His mouth dropped open. "I didn't kill her and I wasn't having an affair. Duncan was the one she was seeing. Not me."

"Really?" Savannah asked with a smile. "Well, isn't that interesting. How long was that going on?"

Todd rolled his eyes. "I don't know. I guess it started a few weeks after we hired Ivy."

"Why the secrecy?" Savannah asked. "Duncan wasn't married."

"Yes, he was," Todd said. "His wife had left him and was asking for a divorce, but he was still married back then. She was demanding full custody of his boys and wanted to move them across the country. Duncan was afraid that if the judge found out about Ivy and her history with the court system that it would be bad for him so he swore me to secrecy. As soon as his divorce was finalized and custody was worked out, he and Ivy were going to get married but then Ivy left."

"Were they fighting before she left?" Arden asked.

"No." He ran a hand through his hair. "At least not that I know of." There was a pause. "No more than most couples."

"Go on," Savannah prompted when he fell silent.

He rolled his eyes again. "She was tired of keeping their relationship a secret and wanted to tell everyone that they were a couple."

"That's why she threw an engagement party," Arden said thoughtfully.

"Yeah."

"That must have made him mad," Paige said.

Shaking his hands at them, Todd said, "Listen, you've got the wrong idea. Duncan would never have hurt that girl. He loved her. If she was murdered like you say, you need to talk to my ex-wife. Wendy threatened to kill Ivy more than once."

"Did she know about Duncan and Ivy?" Savannah asked.

"Only I knew and I only knew because I saw them making out in his truck once."

"Why didn't you tell Wendy about them?" Paige asked. "If she had known maybe she wouldn't have been so convinced you were having an affair with Ivy."

"You don't know Wendy. I'm not kidding when I say she's crazy. You know why I finally left? Because I couldn't take it anymore. About four months ago, Emma woke me up in a panic because she saw someone outside and wanted me to take a look. You know what I saw? My wife out in the backyard, digging her little heart out. Three o'clock in the morning and there she was on her hands and knees in the dirt. She moved my birdbath into the garage and planted her vegetable garden just to get back at me for accidentally knocking over one of her flowerpots. She's vindictive and mean as a snake." He wagged his finger at them. "I'm warning you. Stay away from her."

Chapter 15

It was late in the afternoon by the time they made it back to Arden's house.

Savannah glanced over at Max's house as they climbed out of Paige's car. "I wonder who she is."

Arden glanced toward the blue house as a young woman with short blonde hair and a no nonsense black suit walked out. The woman stopped at the door and looked back inside, a soft smile on her heart shaped face. "See you tonight," she called out before turning and hurrying down the stairs with a happy grin on her face. They watched as she slipped into a black sports car.

Paige said, "I've seen her once or twice. Usually only at night."

"Maybe she's a relative," Savannah said with a hopeful note in her voice.

Paige bit her lip. "I think she might be his girlfriend."

Arden's heart sank. Of course, he has a girlfriend. A man that looked like he did and was as nice as he was wouldn't be single for long.

Noticing Arden's expression, Paige said, "But, she only shows up a couple of times a month, and when he rented the blue house, he said he was single."

"Honey, that status can change on a dime," Savannah said. "Oh well, I wonder if he's found Ivy yet?"

Arden reached into her purse for her house key. "Do you really think he's looking?"

"He's the one who insisted that Ivy was still alive," Savannah said idly.

"I don't think anyone is going to find Ivy." Paige glanced at Arden. "Maybe we should dig up your yard and see if she's buried back there."

Arden unlocked her front door and stepped inside. "I think the killer's already beaten us to that."

"So, do I," Savannah said. "I find it interesting that Wendy decided to do some midnight gardening right around the time you bought your house."

Clover ran across the hardwood floor so fast she couldn't stop in time and slid into Arden's ankles. Arden picked her up and held her close. "I think we should call Emma and see what she says about that. I don't know if I trust Todd."

Savannah seemed surprised. "You think he lied to us?"

"I think he hates Wendy so much that he might say anything. Do you have Emma's cell phone number?"

Savannah pulled out her phone and dialed.

"I believed him," Paige said walking ahead of them towards the living room.

Savannah handed Arden her phone before following Paige.

Arden sighed as her call went straight to voice mail. "Hi Emma, this is Arden. It's urgent that I speak to you. Can you please call me?" She gave her phone number before signing off. When she entered the living room, she discovered Savannah at her kitchen counter and Paige in front of the window.

"Wow!" Paige remarked. "Your yard is shaping up nicely."

Arden smiled, pleased to see the progress Julie was making on her yard. "I can't wait to see when it's finished. Julie's doing such a good job. I really like—" She paused in surprise as Julie appeared at her gate. "Oh, here she comes," she said as Julie opened the gate and made a beeline straight for her back door.

She opened the door and let the girl in. "Hi Julie, I see you got the gate unlocked. That's great!"

"Yeah, I borrowed my uncle's bolt cutters," Julie said in a distracted fashion. "I need to talk to someone."

Arden frowned at the dazed look in Julie's eyes. "Are you alright?"

Julie jerked a thumb over her shoulder. "Yeah I . . ." She paused as though she was confused about something. "Wendy wanted me to plant the oleander bush today so I did."

Arden glanced at her friends then back at the girl not quite understanding why the girl seemed so perplexed. "Was there something wrong with it?"

"No, the bush is fine." She gave them a pained look as she held out her hand. Then slowly uncurling her fingers, she revealed a dirt encrusted charm bracelet in her palm. Her hand was shaking as she dropped the bracelet into Arden's hand. "I think . . . I think this belonged to Ivy."

Savannah and Paige hovered on either side of her as she examined the bracelet.

"I remember her wearing this." Savannah pointed to a cloverleaf charm. "She told me that was the first charm she bought when she arrived here."

Arden looked back up at Julie. "Where did you find this?"

Julie pointed towards Wendy's house. "I was in her yard digging a hole so I could plant that oleander bush and that's when I found it. It was just lying in the dirt." She took a deep breath. "Wendy . . . she got mad at me. She came running out of the house all crazy like yelling at me. Told me that I was digging in the wrong place and made me fill the hole back up and move the oleander bush a few feet away."

"Did she see the bracelet?" Arden asked.

"No, I stuck it in my pocket and then did as she wanted." A look of concern crossed her face. "Why would Ivy's bracelet be buried in Wendy's yard?"

Playing devil's advocate, Arden said, "Ivy may have lost it when she was working over there."

Julie didn't seem convinced by Arden's suggestion. "It wasn't lying on the ground like it had fallen off her wrist. It was buried. *Deep.*"

Savannah reacted as though she had just won the lottery. "Woo hoo! That's it! That's the evidence we need!" She reached for the phone on the kitchen counter. "Let's call the police."

Arden took the phone out of her hand and replaced it back in its cradle. "What good will that do? They're not going to march over there and start digging without a warrant and I doubt they'll get one just because of this," she said holding the charm bracelet up, "may have once belonged to Ivy. Knowing our luck, someone will tip Wendy off and she'll just move the body."

"Body?" Julie's eyes widened and her face lost all color. "Oh boy."

Arden helped the young girl sit down before she passed out. "It's all right, Julie, just breathe."

"But I didn't find a body," Julie insisted. "Just the bracelet."

Savannah opened the refrigerator and helped herself to a soft drink. "That just means that you either didn't dig deep enough or wide enough." She took a sip, before adding, "I think poor Ivy's nothing but bones by now."

Arden felt sick. She knew Ivy was dead but it still saddened her to think she had been unceremoniously dumped into someone's backyard. She glanced at Paige and could tell by the expression on her face she was thinking the same thing.

Paige, her eyes round and filled with disgust, pointed towards Wendy's house. "Wait a second," Paige said her voice filling with horror. "Do you mean to tell me Ivy's buried underneath Wendy's vegetable garden? The same garden where she grew the cucumbers we ate for lunch?" She clutched her stomach. "I think I'm going to be sick."

"Take deep breaths, honey." Savannah told Paige before walking over to the kitchen table. "Julie, your uncle is taking Wendy to a concert tonight. Do you know what time they're leaving?"

"Around nine?"

"Any idea when they'll be back?"

Julie shrugged. "They're not going to be back before late. Eleven, I think."

Savannah stepped into the sunroom and gazed up through the glass towards the purple house with a smile. "That gives us two hours, ladies."

A clammy feeling came over Arden at the look in Savannah's eyes. "For what?"

Turning her attention towards Julie, Savannah grinned. "Do you mind if we borrow your shovel, Julie?"

Julie's eyes widened. "Oh boy."

166

The Perfect Recipe for Murder

Chapter 16

Oddly enough, Arden reflected several hours later, all the times she had fantasized about moving to Cloverleaf Cove, she couldn't remember a one that consisted of her sneaking out of her house under the cover of darkness along with two of her neighbors to dig up a dead body. Nevertheless, to her surprise, that's exactly what she was doing and she was enjoying every minute of it. The planning, plotting and secrecy of the operation excited her. Far more than it should but she didn't have the luxury of worrying about it.

Time was running out. In less than twenty-four hours, Bruce would be cremated and any hope of proving he was murdered would be lost.

Therefore, as soon as Wendy and Duncan left that night, Arden, Paige and Savannah crossed Arden's backyard, slipped through the newly unlocked gate and then quickly and quietly walked along the brick walkway to Wendy's backyard.

Staring down at the vegetable garden, Arden slipped a pair of gloves out of her jeans and slipped them on. "Are you ready?"

"I'm ready," Paige said tugging a black knit cap down over her hair.

Savannah reached into the bag she was carrying and pulled out a walkie-talkie which she handed to Paige. "Then let's get started."

Paige looked at the walkie-talkie as if she had never seen one before. "What's this for?"

"Well, honey," Savannah said sweetly, "someone has to keep lookout."

A smile broke across Paige's face. "Okay."

"So," Savannah continued, "I was thinking that since I'm the oldest that it should be me."

Paige's smile fell. "Oh." Her lips quirked up. "Somehow, I knew when you trotted over here in those black high heels you weren't going to be doing any digging tonight."

Savannah pressed a hand to her heart. "Oh darlin', if it weren't for my bad back I would be down in the dirt with you."

Arden and Paige exchanged an amused glance. "If you're not going to be here with us, where are you going to be?" Arden asked as she braided her hair.

Savannah walked toward the porch, reached up and unscrewed the lightbulb by the door. "At the entrance gate."

"That's not going to give us much of a warning," Arden said picking up the shovel and sticking it into the ground.

"Don't worry." Savannah walked along the porch and unscrewed the other light. "I handed Julie her own walkie-talkie and stationed her in my tower. She'll keep watch on the main road and let us know if her uncle and Wendy come home early."

A rumble of thunder sounded in the distance.

Glancing up at the sky with a worried frown, Paige stuck her palm out. "If Julie is keeping watch why are you leaving?"

"Two eyes are better than one," Savannah said. "If she looks away at the wrong moment, we're sunk."

Arden arched an eyebrow. "So, you're the lookout for our lookout?"

Savannah beamed as she walked to the lanterns on top of the columns. "That's right."

Paige frowned as Savannah reached up and unscrewed the lantern lightbulbs. "How are we going to see without lights?"

"Easy." Savannah reached into her bag and pulled out a small lantern. "Now, make sure to use our call signs," she said turning on the lantern and setting it on the ground next to the vegetable garden. "We don't want anyone to overhear and figure out who we are." She reached into her bag and pulled out another walkie-talkie. "Now, I've made sure to silence the beeps so don't worry about them making any noises." Handing Arden the walkie-talkie, she smiled encouragingly at them both. "Okay, Sherbet, Flamingo, let me know the moment you find Ivy."

"I want a new call sign," Arden called out as Savannah slipped back through the gate.

Paige held a finger to her lip. "Shh." She stuck her shovel into the dirt then glanced up at the sky again. "We better hurry. It looks like it's going to start raining soon."

Determined to find Ivy before it started to rain or Wendy came home and caught them, Paige and Arden worked as quickly as possible only stopping when Savannah interrupted them an hour later.

"Car's coming," Savannah said causing Arden's heart to pound.

Checking her watch, she pulled up out of the hole she and Paige had dug and picked up the walkie-talkie. "It can't be them. It's too early."

A second later, Savannah responded with a relieved sigh. "Oh no, you're right, Sherbet. It's just Silver Fox and that girl we saw leaving his house earlier. We need a name for her."

"Speaking of names," Arden said, "I want a new call sign, Jolly Green Giant."

"Later, keep digging."

Arden dropped the walkie-talkie onto the ground and stepped back into the ever-deepening hole next to her. She wiggled her fingers which had tightened over the shovel for a few seconds. Then blowing out her breath, she started to dig once again. Less than a minute later, she paused as a feeling of unease swept over her, causing her hair to stand on end. Licking her lips, she turned and stared at Wendy's house, her gaze sweeping along the windows, searching for something.

Breathing heavily, Paige stopped and looked up at her. "What's wrong?"

Arden ran a hand over the back of her neck trying to dispel the creepy feeling she was getting. "Do you ever get the feeling you're being watched?" she asked as she slipped off her jacket and laid it down on the ground. She tried dusting off the dirt on her black tank top and jeans but quickly gave up, her attention once more returning to the purple house. "There's no one there, but I can't get past this feeling that someone's there."

Paige groaned. "Don't tell me that." She reached for the walkie-talkie. "I probably should have mentioned this before, Jolly Green Giant, but if we get caught, I'm out of here and I don't know you people."

Taking one last look at the house, Arden forced her unease to the back of her mind as she resumed digging.

A few minutes later, Paige stuck her shovel in the ground and shook her head. "Ivy's not here."

Arden grunted as her shovel hit a tree root. She wiped a hand across her forehead. "She's got to be. All the clues point to her being right here."

Julie's voice suddenly broke through the quiet. "Uh, I don't remember what I'm supposed to call you all but . . . I think they're back." There was a moment's silence then. "Yep, that's my uncle's truck."

Paige sharply sucked in her breath. Wasting no time, she hopped out of the hole and began furiously shoveling dirt back into the hole. "Hurry."

Deciding to follow her example, Arden laid her shovel down and started to step up and out but to her surprise, something kept her left foot from moving.

"Okay ladies," Savannah said. "Time to get a move on. I see their headlights."

Arden glanced down at her foot which had become wedged underneath the root and the dirt Paige was hurriedly tossing into the hole. "Paige stop!"

Paige froze. "What's wrong?"

Arden reached down towards her boot and tugged. "I'm stuck. I think one of my boot laces is caught on a root."

Paige's eyes widened in horror. "What?"

"Um, yeah," Julie said, "they just turned down the street and . . . they're now pulling into Wendy's driveway. Can I come down now?"

"Ladies," Savannah said, "if you haven't already done so, now would be a good time to skedaddle out of there."

Paige scrambled over to her walkie-talkie. "Sherbet's stuck."

Tugging off her gloves, Arden sat down and tried to untie her bootlaces. She glanced up as the house lights came on. "Paige, how are we going to explain this?"

Arden jerked her head up at the sound of a gate banging shut. She looked around surprised to find herself alone. "Paige?"

Paige's voice came over walkie-talkie. "I'm so sorry, Sherbet. I promise I'll make this up to you someday. Please don't rat me out."

"Of course, she won't," Savannah responded soothingly. "We all knew the risk we were taking. Sherbet, I just want you to know that if *you know who* wasn't up for re-election I would be more than happy to go to jail with you, but unfortunately, she can't afford the scandal right now. My daughter-in-law may be a witch but she's our witch. But I promise the next time something like this happens I will stand by your side."

Arden grabbed the walkie-talkie. "What next time?" She glanced back at the house as the kitchen light came on. Reaching behind her, she flipped off the lantern, and then returned her attention back to her boot. She managed to work her foot out only a few seconds before the back door opened and the screen door creaked open.

With no other place to hide available, Arden fell back into the hole and laid down praying Wendy and Duncan couldn't see her or the mess in the yard.

"Yeah, you're right. All your lights are out back here," Duncan said. "I'll check the breaker."

She heard a pair of heels clicking against the patio. "Don't bother," Wendy said. "I already did. I told Emma to change these lights."

"She must have forgotten."

"She was probably too busy talking," Wendy said, annoyance coloring her voice.

"You shouldn't have fired her."

"Why not?"

"Honey, where is she going to go? You should have at least given her time to get another job. People are going to talk."

"I couldn't care less." There was a pause then, "I had to let her go. She talks too much."

There was a moment of silence, then a suddenly rumble of thunder.

Perfect, Arden thought as a raindrop hit her forehead. Just perfect.

The doorbell rang then. Over and over and over until Wendy finally said, "Who could that be?"

The screen door creaked open then banged shut.

Arden wanted to lift her head and take a look but she didn't dare. For all she knew, Duncan was still standing on the patio.

A flash of lightning and a rumble of thunder caught her attention. She closed her eyes just as a giant raindrop landed on her forehead.

Maybe Max was right. Maybe she did need a hobby.

She was contemplating joining that cooking class Wendy had mentioned when she heard Savannah and Paige's voices.

She breathed out a sigh of relief and then smiled. The cavalry had finally arrived.

She knew they wouldn't leave her behind.

Hearing the sound of the screen door opening, and then shutting, followed by the sound of the back door closing, Arden lifted her head. She peeked over the grass towards the house.

Duncan and Wendy stood with their backs to the kitchen window. Savannah and Paige stood across from them and from the amount of hand gestures her friends were doing, she had a feeling they were trying to get Duncan and Wendy to follow them, apparently without much success.

It didn't matter. All Arden needed was a distraction. She braced herself, preparing to jump up, grab her things and race for the gate, but the sound of a sharp bark followed by the creak of the gate stopped her.

Oh, please no!

She dropped her head back down and laid as still as she could as the sound of panting and dog tags jangling against one another came closer.

She squeezed her eyes shut, praying she wasn't about to be caught.

Please. Please. Please.

She reluctantly pried her eyes open as a cold wet nose pressed against her forehead. A slobbery kiss came next.

Lucky barked down at her in excitement, his whole body shaking along with his tail.

"Shh. Lucky. Go," she whispered which only encouraged the puppy into barking louder.

Max came into view next. Towering over her, he smiled at her in amusement. "So, I was out walking Lucky when I ran into Savannah and Paige. They said something about rescuing you before marching up to Wendy's door. Do I even want to ask what you three are up to?"

She swiped away another raindrop from her cheek. "I can explain."

"Oh, I'm sure you can."

"Are they watching?"

He glanced toward the house. "No."

She started to rise up but to her surprise, Max quickly scooped Lucky up in his arms and dropped into the hole beside her.

He wrapped his arms around her and held her close as the back door opened.

She laid a hand against his chest, trying to put some distance between them, but he held her tight. "I don't think your girlfriend is going to like this," she whispered.

His brow furrowed as he looked at her. "I don't have a girlfriend."

The screen door creaked open.

"It's late, Savannah," Wendy said, "and so far, you haven't explained why either one of us should go out front."

"Look," Duncan said, "I'll go."

"Well," Paige said, trying to sound upbeat, "We really would like to show both of you."

Light suddenly spilled out onto the ground.

"There was nothing wrong with this bulb," Wendy said with a confused tone of voice. "It just wasn't screwed in tightly."

"How very odd," Savannah said. "You know the same thing happened at my house once."

More light appeared above them. "This one wasn't screwed in either," Wendy said. "Duncan, go over to those lanterns—"

"I just wanted to apologize to you, Wendy," Savannah interrupted her voice sounding desperate. "We should never have suspected you."

"Suspected Wendy?" Duncan asked sharply. "Of what?"

"Never you mind," Wendy said just as sharply. "Well, thank you, Savannah. Paige. That's nice of you to say. Why don't we talk about this at granddad's funeral?"

"Speaking of which," Duncan said. "You do know that the funeral isn't until tomorrow, don't you?"

Savannah's voice sounded confused. "Well, of course we do."

"Then why are you two dressed all in black now?" Duncan asked.

"We're in mourning," Savannah responded, her voice breaking. "Bruce's death affected us deeper than you know."

"I'm sure," Wendy said dryly. "Where's Arden?"

Arden cringed at the mention of her name, then cringed again as it began to rain in earnest.

There was a pause. Then Savannah said, "She's a little under the weather at the moment."

Max snorted in amusement. He wrapped his arms around Arden and Lucky, holding them close as the rain soaked them through and through.

Arden pushed her hair off her face and stared at Max's handsome face. His lips twitched and before she knew it, she was smothering her face into his shirt to keep from laughing at the ridiculousness of it all. She barely noticed the door shutting and everything going silent around them as he gathered her close to his body.

"I think they've gone inside," he whispered into her ear.

Reluctantly, Arden lifted her head off of Max's chest and looked over at the house. She spotted Wendy at the kitchen sink looking out and ducked back down. Resting her head on his chest again, she asked, "What are we going to do?"

"Drown." He paused for a second then said, "What makes you think I have a girlfriend?"

She pushed against his chest again. "I saw a girl leave your place this afternoon."

He cupped her hand to his chest. "That's just Dana. She's a co-worker of mine. That's all."

Arden felt a surge of happiness. "Your co-worker? Well, I—" She frowned. "You're a writer. Isn't that usually a solitary job?"

Max shifted his position, curling her into his side as he peeked over the grass. "Yes, but I have an editor and a publisher and an assistant. It's not as solitary as you might think."

Smiling, Arden relaxed against him. She laid her head on his chest, waiting for a sign that it was safe to escape. Although, if she were honest, she'd have to admit that she did rather enjoy the feeling of his strong arms around her. Lucky's fur tickled her nose and she wrinkled her nose. The wet dog she could probably do without, but other than that and the torrential downpour, being in Max's arms wasn't so bad.

She wasn't sure how much time had passed as they laid there together, but eventually, the rain slowed and then stopped.

Wendy's back door opened a few seconds later and heavy steps echoed over the patio followed by a pair of high heels.

"The rain finally let up," Duncan said. "You know that was weird. I didn't think we'd ever get rid of them."

"They're up to something," Wendy said. "I bet you they're the ones who unscrewed the light bulbs."

Duncan laughed. "Don't be ridiculous. Why would they do that?"

Wendy mumbled something unintelligible.

Duncan cleared his throat. "If you would let me, I could put a gazebo right over there."

Wendy sighed. "Yes, I know. You've mentioned it several times."

"I just want to give you something nice."

"A pool would be nice."

"Now we're talking," Duncan said enthusiastically. "Come here, I've been wanting to do this all night."

Arden looked over at Max's face only inches from hers and blushed as Wendy and Duncan began to kiss. The intensity of Max's gaze caught hers causing her nerve endings to tingle. Her gaze dropped to his mouth as he leaned forward.

"Does this mean you're going to marry me?" Duncan asked.

"No," Wendy said sharply, causing Max to turn his attention back to the other couple. "I haven't made up my mind yet. I wish you would stop asking me. I'll let you know when I'm ready."

"Well, don't take my head off. What's wrong, sweetheart? You've been acting as if you're mad at me all night. What did I do?"

"I'm not mad. I was just thinking that maybe we shouldn't cremate granddad. He never spoke about what he wanted, but I was thinking it might be nice to bury him next to my grandmother."

Arden's eyebrows rose. That was a surprise. She would have thought Wendy would be desperate to cremate Bruce now that she knew they were on to her.

"We talked about this, honey," Duncan said sounding a bit desperate. "Bruce told me before he died that it's what he wanted."

"When did he tell you that? He never mentioned it to me. You know, I stopped by my grandmother's grave today. There's a place for him there. He obviously intended to be buried next to her when she died. Why would he change his mind?"

Arden frowned. This wasn't right. If Wendy had poisoned her grandfather, she should be pushing to have Bruce cremated not arguing against doing it.

"I don't know," Duncan said. "But he did want to be cremated. He told me so himself."

"Why tell you?" Wendy asked her voice suspicious. "He didn't like you."

"That's not true. We were friends once."

There was a pause then Wendy said, "I'm going to tell the funeral home that I've changed my mind."

Duncan's voice hardened. "No, that's not a good idea, sweetheart."

Arden exchanged a glance with Max.

"Why?" Wendy asked.

"I just think we should honor your grandfather's last wishes. We've already decided he's going to be cremated and that's that. Trust me, Wendy, it's for the best."

"Take your hands off me," Wendy snapped.

Max tensed under her arms. He craned his neck to look over the edge of the hole.

"Honey," Duncan whined.

"Don't honey me," Wendy said. "I know what you're doing. You think I killed him."

There was a moment of silence then, "No. No, of course not." More silence. "Did you?"

Wendy made a note of disgust in her voice.

A few seconds later, the back door opened and then slammed shut causing Lucky to howl in surprise.

She and Max waited breathlessly for a moment, and then cringed at the same time as Duncan whistled.

"Lucky? Is that you? Come here, boy."

Max held Lucky tight as Duncan continued to call the dog's name. His heavy footsteps pounded against the patio as he neared, stopping only when his cell phone rang.

Arden breathed a sigh of relief and felt Max do the same.

"Hello?" Duncan's voice suddenly grew rough with anger. "No, listen to me, keep everyone away from there. Tell the Mayor to stop worrying. I'm not going to leave a gaping hole in the park. It'll be finished tomorrow." He sighed in frustration. "No, I don't want you to go. I am in charge. You tell the Mayor—never mind. I'll talk to the Mayor. You just keep everyone away from there." He cursed softly as he stomped towards the house and then through the door.

Max lifted his head. "Okay, let's go."

As nice as it was being held by Max, Arden didn't need to be told twice. She grabbed the walkie-talkie, the lantern, her jacket and her boot. Then she scrambled out of the hole and towards the gate as fast as she could with Max and Lucky at her side.

Chapter 17

Once on the brick walkway between her house and the bluffs, Arden hopped along on one foot trying her best to slip into her boot. Max stood beside her, one hand on her elbow to steady her, the other at her hip. She relaxed against him, partly for warmth, and partly because she liked the feel of him at her side.

She did another little hop as she tried to force her wet sock into her boot. Realizing it wasn't going to work, she reluctantly moved out of Max's embrace and sat down on the short brick wall on the other side of the walkway. She tried to ignore the fact that there was a sheer drop to the beach on the other side of the wall and focused on wringing the water out of her sock. Max leaned a hip against the wall and stared out at the ocean while she slipped her sock and her boot back on.

She had just started to reach for her bootlaces when Lucky jumped up, grabbed a loose bootlace between his teeth, and began playing tug of war.

"Do you want to tell me what you three were up to now?" Max asked.

"What do you mean by 'we three'?" she asked after finally getting her shoestring out of Lucky's mouth. She scratched the wet puppy behind his ear then hopped down. "Did you see anyone else in that hole with me?"

Max reached into a pocket at the side of his thigh and pulled out a thin blue leash which he attached to Lucky's collar. "It's no secret that you three have been stirring things up in town." He straightened. "You've been asking a lot of questions since you've moved to town and people are noticing."

Sticking the walkie-talkie under one arm, she grabbed the lantern and set off toward her gate. "How else are we going to figure out who killed Bruce and Ivy? We're really close to figuring out what happened. We've got motive, means, opportunity . . . We just need proof."

He took her elbow again as they hurried walked down the brick pathway to her gate. "This isn't one of your mystery games."

"I know that," she said. "Those were much easier." She looked down at her dirty clothes. "Cleaner too."

He stopped and turned to face her. "I'm serious. This person has already killed twice. If they think you're close to figuring out who they are, you could find yourself joining Bruce and Ivy."

Prepared to argue her point, she was momentarily taken aback by his statement. "You believe Ivy was murdered now?"

"I think you're right and something did happen to her," he added reluctantly as he ushered her through her gate. "I'm just not sure what. I managed to track down her foster sister. The last time she heard from Ivy was about a month before she disappeared. They had made plans to celebrate Ivy's birthday in November but Ivy never showed."

Arden held up her finger. "Aha! See, just more proof that she's still here somewhere."

The corners of his lips turned up as he plucked a leaf from her braid. "In Wendy's garden?"

"Well, apparently no, but she's somewhere around here." Arden ran her fingers over her wet hair, cringing at the dirt and mud caked to the back of her head. She could just imagine how she looked.

Max stepped in front of her giving her a good look of his back. She fought the urge to laugh, noting the amount of mud on the back of his shirt and khaki pants. She cleared her throat, amusement bubbling up. "I should probably thank you for not giving me away back there. If you want to give me a dry cleaning bill I wouldn't blame you."

He glanced over his shoulder at her for a moment before pulling at his shirt trying to assess the damage to his clothes. "Well, it's not a total loss." He grinned. "I've been wanting to get to know my new neighbor better anyway."

Blushing, she reached into her pocket and pulled out her key as they neared her patio. Searching for a safer topic of conversation she said, "I don't know what we're going to do about Wendy's garden. I hope she's the forgiving sort."

"If she did kill Ivy and her grandfather, I'd say your hope is misplaced."

"We were so certain Ivy was buried there, it didn't occur to us that she wouldn't be," she said before going on to describe their conversation with Todd Grayson.

"I doubt you'll find any trace of Ivy now. If she was killed and her body moved, the killer more than likely disposed of her in the ocean." He stuck his hands into his pockets. "Just a box of bones now. Much easier to get rid of."

She bit her lip. It hadn't occurred to her that killer might have disposed of Ivy's bones in the ocean. "Why wouldn't the killer do that five years ago? Why wait?"

"We don't know that they didn't. But just for argument sake, one reason might be that they couldn't get the body down the bluff without being caught. They'd have to carry it out to the walkway and either down the stairs or throw it over the bluff. Then they would have to drag it out to the ocean. More chance of discovery that way. If they waited until there was nothing left but bones, they could just box her up and carry her out."

The wind blew through causing her to shiver and the wind chimes to chime. She sighed wearily. "Then she's gone."

"More than likely but . . ."

"But?"

"Duncan seemed pretty anxious about something tonight," he added almost reluctantly.

She started to agree when she noticed a wasp just above her head. "I need to get rid of those wasps."

"Hornets."

"Well, whatever they are, I want them gone." She pushed open the door and held it open for him, expecting him to follow her inside.

He shook his head. "I think I might go take a walk."

She glanced up as thunder rumbled and lightning streaked across the sky. Her brow furrowed. "Now?"

"Yeah, I think I might go take a look at the park. See what got Duncan so upset."

She set the walkie-talkie and the lantern on the kitchen island, and then stepped back out. "I'll go with you," she said eagerly.

He smiled. "I'm just going to go poking around."

"Yeah but—"

The doorbell rang interrupting her. "Who in the world could that be?" she asked glancing down at her watch.

Lucky lifted his ears and growled low in his throat.

A hiss and a yowl of protest drew Arden's attention down. Clover, her hair standing straight up stood by Arden's feet, clearly not happy with having an interloper in her backyard. Staring the puppy down, she growled low in her throat.

"It's probably your partners in crime." Max backed up, dragging Lucky with him, whose full attention was now focused on the kitten. "Tell you what? If I do find something, you will be the first person I call."

"Promise?"

"Promise." He waved as he slipped out and disappeared behind the hedge at the side of her house.

The doorbell rang again. Arden kicked off her muddy boots, stepped inside and hurried towards the front door, with Clover hot on her heels. "Coming."

The walkie-talkie suddenly sprang to life. "Sherbet," Savannah said, "just hang tight. Flamingo and I have a plan."

She glanced over her shoulder towards the walkie-talkie as she hurried to the front door. Figuring that it was Savannah and Paige on the other side of the door, she unlocked the door. "What happened over at Wendy's?" she asked as she opened the door.

Emma Varner stood on the other side. "She fired me."

Arden's mouth hung open in surprise. "Emma?"

Emma took that as an invitation to walk in. "She told me that I wasn't welcome anymore." Standing in the foyer, she twisted her handbag in her hands. "I didn't expect to stay there forever. I knew after Bruce died that I'd have to leave. Lord knows she told me as much several times in the last couple of months, but I at least thought she'd give me a week or two to find something else." The older lady plastered a smile to her face. "Oh well, can't cry about it. What's done is done." She gasped in shock as she looked at Arden from the top of her head down to her feet. "Oh, my goodness. Look at you."

Arden self-consciously glanced down at her muddy jacket, tank top and jeans.

"You're soaking wet," Emma said. "Honey, did you get caught out in the rain?"

"Come in, Sherbet!" Savannah called from the walkie-talkie. "I certainly hope you didn't drown out there."

Arden glanced from Emma to the walkie-talkie as the former continued talking.

"You should go change before you catch your death of cold." Emma's features softened in concern. "Did you fall too? Honey, you're just covered in mud. What in the world happened to you? Are you okay?"

Arden nodded automatically, her attention divided between Savannah and Emma. She held up her finger as she started backing up.

"Anyway, I came as soon as I got your call tonight," Emma said as she followed her towards the kitchen. "Is that Savannah calling for sherbet? Personally, I like ice cream myself."

A small meow caught Emma's attention. Her face broke out in a beaming smile as she stared down at Clover. "Oh, what a pretty kitty." She bent over and held out her hand for Clover to sniff. "I love cats. Wendy hated cats. She hated all animals." Her gaze swung to the windows with a frown as it began to rain once again. "Oh, I hope it doesn't rain very long. I've got such a long drive. My vision isn't what it used to be. It's so hard to see at night now, but it's especially bad in the rain."

"Sherbet!" Paige said her tone becoming desperate. "Are you there? I swear, Jolly Green Giant, if she doesn't answer, I'm marching back over there. I don't care what the Wicked Witch says."

"My daughter-in-law?" Savannah asked, her voice sounding confused.

"No," Paige said. "You know who. Barney doesn't fit anymore so I came up with a new name for the house. I think it fits."

"That doesn't work," Savannah said. "It has to be a color."

"Barney wasn't a color."

"Yes, it was," Savannah countered. "Everyone associates the name Barney with the color purple. It's a well-known fact that Barney means purple."

"No, it's doesn't."

"Yes, it does."

"Barney does not mean--Look, can we discuss this after we've rescued Sherbet, please?"

Arden hurried over to the walkie-talkie. "It's okay. I'm back home."

"Oh, thank goodness," Paige said. "I was starting to get worried."

"How did you escape?" Savannah asked.

"Ma--" She glanced back at Emma. "The Silver Fox rescued me."

"Oohh," Paige cooed, "do tell."

"I'll fill you in later," Arden said glancing back at Emma.

"I don't suppose you two found Ivy?" Paige asked.

Emma's head rose. "Ivy? Ivy Kent? Is she back?"

"Emma's here," Arden said. "I'll call you all in little while. Sherbet out." She set the walkie-talkie back down and walked over to the living room where Emma was waiting with Clover snuggled on her lap and purring loudly.

Before she could say anything, there was a knock on the French doors to her left.

Julie stood on the patio looking in, out of breath and panting. "Hey, is everything okay?" she asked as Arden opened the door. The young woman glanced over at Emma in surprise. "Oh hey, Mrs. Varner."

"Everything's fine, Julie," Arden said. "You didn't have to run over here."

"I was getting worried about you." She glanced up as thunder boomed overhead and lightning flashed across the sky. "I checked the weather. It's going to be bad tonight." She looked uncomfortable as she glanced from Arden to Emma and back again. "Um, my uncle's not back tonight and . . ." Her voice dropped to a whisper. "I'm kind of spooked what with all this murder talk." She glanced up again as thunder shook the house and the lights flickered. "The storm's not helping either. Do you mind if I stay over here with you until he gets back?"

Arden immediately nodded. Truth was she was kind of spooked too and would feel better with some more company. She welcomed the girl in and told her to make herself comfortable.

Within minutes, Julie was sprawled out on the couch with her phone in her hands.

Emma looked up expectantly as Arden walked into the living room. "I got your message and came right away, dear. What was it that you want to talk to me about?"

Deciding that it might be best to question Emma alone, Arden suggested they move to the library. Figures, dressed in black and burying bodies in the backyard was the stuff of nightmares, and she didn't want to upset Julie more than she already was.

Once Emma was up with Clover safely ensconced in her arms, Arden turned her attention to Julie. "Julie, help yourself to anything in the kitchen. Emma and I will be in the library if you need anything."

Julie was focused on whatever was on her phone, barely paying attention as the two older women excused themselves. Without looking up from her phone, she gave a half-hearted wave and muttered, "Thanks," as she adjusted the pillows behind her head.

Arden led Emma down the back hallway and into the library. She wasn't about to sit down or touch anything in the state she was in so she settled for crossing her arms and hovering nearby while Emma took a seat in one of the comfy reading chairs with Clover nestled in her lap.

As soon as Emma was settled, Arden wasted no time getting to the reason why she called Emma, focusing first on the figure she supposedly saw in Wendy's yard the night before Todd left for good.

"Scared me half to death." Emma said her voice dropping to a whisper. "I couldn't tell who it was. I thought that maybe I was seeing things. It was misty outside, and if there's no moon out, it can get pretty dark in that backyard. So, I went and woke Todd up so he could take a look. He said it was Wendy."

"What made him say that? Did he go outside?"

"No, he recognized her on account of Bruce's raincoat." She smiled. "Bruce loved that raincoat. Had it for years. Todd liked it because it was easy to spot Bruce in a crowd when he was wearing it. See, Bruce knocked over a paint can from the shelf in the garage a few years ago and splattered the back of his coat with this periwinkle blue color. It was a real pretty color. I ended up using that same color in my bedroom. It's a really nice soft color. Goes with a lot of things."

"Uh huh, so if it was Bruce's raincoat, why did Todd automatically assume it was Wendy outside?"

"Because Bruce was sound asleep. I know because I checked in on him just before I saw her outside in the yard. It had to be her. Wendy sometimes borrowed her grandpa's raincoat when she had to dash out for something and it was raining."

"Could you tell what she was doing?"

"It looked like she was planting something. There was this box next to her and I could see her lift something out—couldn't tell what it was—but I saw her hand move and then place whatever it was in the ground." She shivered. "Gave me the heebie-jeebies." She glanced up as thunder shook the house. "This weather is something, huh?"

Arden was more concerned about Wendy's reaction than the thunder at the moment. "Did you ask Wendy about it the next day?"

"Of course." She pursed her lips together. "She told me I must have been dreaming."

"Did you ever take a look to see what she had buried?"

Emma shook her head. "Wendy doesn't like people fussing in her garden."

191

Arden started to sit but remembering the state of her clothes jumped up at the last second. "Did you tell Bruce what you saw?"

Nodding, Emma ran her hand down Clover's back. "He said that it couldn't have been Wendy."

"Why not?"

"I don't think he had a reason. I suppose he didn't want to admit that his granddaughter's a little nutty. He was real interested in what I saw until I mentioned that I thought it was her. Then he didn't want to talk about it. Just said it wasn't her."

Arden bit her lip, thinking. "Did you know Ivy and Duncan were engaged to be married?"

Emma's eyes widened. "You're kidding? Boy, they kept that one a secret, didn't they?" Her brow furrowed as she tilted her head to the side. "I guess that explains why I kept seeing Ivy sneaking over to his house at all hours of the night. I just thought she was visiting Julie. I can see why he kept it a secret though. He and Claire— that was his wife's name—were separated and going through a nasty divorce when Ivy came to town. If Claire had found out about Ivy, she probably would have used that in the divorce. You know my husband used to work for Duncan and Claire before he died. That's how I came to be here. Duncan put in a good word for me with Todd and he offered me a job after Wendy fired Ivy."

"That was nice of him. What happened between Duncan and his wife?"

She shrugged. "I guess they just fell out of love. Things hadn't been good for a while. I believe money was tight for far too many years and that caused a lot of friction between them. They fought over money a lot and

. . ." She sighed. "Well, when Julie arrived seven years ago, it created even more of a strain on their marriage."

"Why?"

"After Julie's folks died in a car accident, Duncan brought her home and began raising her as if she was his own daughter. It wasn't long after Julie arrived that Claire filed for divorce. I guess Julie moving in was the straw that broke the camel's back, as they say. Claire just resented Julie so much that she left. She took their two boys and moved to Arizona to live with her parents six months later."

"I guess teenage girls can be rather expensive to take care of, especially if the family is already struggling."

"I don't think that was it. Duncan inherited some money from his brother and he was put in charge of the trust they left for Julie so it's not like money was a problem by the time she moved in. I think Claire resented all the attention Duncan was paying Julie. I never understood what Claire expected him to do. Julie was an orphan. Duncan's a bit self-absorbed at times but he's a good guy. When he wants to be, of course." She smiled down at Clover as the kitten stretched out on her lap. "I used to have a cat. Her name was Molly." She glanced up as the grandfather clock in the hall chimed. With a regretful sigh, she stood. "I should probably get going." She placed Clover in Arden's arms. "Last time it stormed this hard, the highway got flooded."

Arden was reluctant to let her leave. She followed Emma to the front door, her conscience nagging her to do something as Emma opened the door. The rain was coming down hard now and she worried about the older woman driving in the downpour. "Maybe you should wait until the storm passes over."

"It's supposed to last all night. Best I go ahead and go now. Don't worry. I'll be fine."

Arden looked out towards the street where Emma's beat up old clunker sat under the street lamp. The old car looked like it was ready to fall apart.

Emma lifted up the hood of her raincoat. "Well, goodnight." She paused, her brow furrowing. "Why was it so urgent to talk to me tonight?"

"I spoke to Todd Grayson today and he told me about the figure digging in your backyard. Bruce had mentioned seeing something similar and I wanted to talk to you to see if it was true."

Emma snorted in amusement. "Oh, I doubt Bruce actually saw anything. He was probably just passing my story off as his. He liked getting attention." She smiled as she reached out to scratch Clover underneath her chin. "How is Todd doing? I miss him a lot. It just wasn't the same when he moved out."

"He's doing well." She glanced down as Clover leaned into Emma's hand. "I heard he took you to the emergency room the day Ivy . . . disappeared."

She smiled. "He's such a sweet man. Spent the whole afternoon with me." She lifted a hand to her face. "You should have seen me. I looked like such a fright. My face was all swollen."

"What happened?"

"I was over here helping Ivy clean up after her party. Bless her heart; she wasn't much of a housekeeper. We were cleaning up the yard when she took a broom and went after a hornet's nest. It fell right smack dab on my head." She chuckled good-naturedly. "I could have killed her. She did her best to help. Got stung a few places herself, but I got the worse of it though." Her eyes lit up in amusement. "You should have seen the look on Todd's face when he saw me. He insisted on driving me to the hospital right then and there. I told him it wasn't necessary, but I guess I looked so bad he didn't want to take any chances. It was probably for the best. I was feeling kind of funny."

Arden frowned. Something Emma had just said tugged at her. A vague memory of something someone had said recently hovered just out of reach and no matter how hard she tried to recall the memory, it stayed frustratingly out of focus. Pushing it aside for the moment, she asked, "Was there anyone else helping clean up that day?"

Arden looked thoughtful. "No, just me and Ivy."

"Did you see anyone over here?"

Emma slowly shook her head.

"Did you see Ivy again after that?"

"No, she was gone by the time we got home." She sighed. "We didn't find out she had stolen anything until Gladys Oakley returned home."

They glanced up as the lights began to flicker again.

Emma sighed again. "That's my cue to go, I'm afraid."

"What will you do now?" Arden asked.

"Oh, I'll find something. I—" She faltered as her tears sprung to her eyes. ". . . It's hard right now. I don't have much in savings." She smiled through her tears. "But I'll be fine though. I always bounce back."

A painful lump formed in Arden's throat. Frightening memories of being alone with little money came back all of the sudden and to her surprise she found herself saying, "Why don't you come work for me?"

Emma's eyebrows rose.

"I need help with taking care of this place. I hate dusting and I'm a horrible cook. I could probably use a little help. Maybe a few hours a week. On a trial basis, of course. You could live here until you get on your feet."

Emma's face lit up. She enveloped Arden into a sudden bear hug cutting off her oxygen. "You won't regret this." She leaned back with a brilliant smile on her face. "I can cook, clean, take out the trash, wash the windows. Oh, thank you! Thank you so much!"

Arden's cell phone suddenly rang interrupting Emma. Excusing herself, she set Clover on the floor, and then walked back to the library.

Max was on the other end of the line.

"Did you find anything?" she asked, closing the library door behind her.

"No, sorry," he said disappointment coloring his voice. "It seems they were worried about the site flooding where they're going to put the fountain. It's basically a pool right now. Duncan put a tarp over it and then got into his car and drove away."

"But what if . . ." She glanced at the door. She could have sworn she heard a floorboard creak. "What if Ivy's buried underneath there?"

"She's not. I know because I checked myself as soon as he left. There's nothing there. You should see my clothes now. You know there is one thing wrong with your theory."

"What?"

"Well, if the killer is the same person who stole Paige's boots, then that leaves out Duncan. I don't think they're his style."

"I thought of that. He could have an accomplice. Wendy for instance."

"Based on their conversation tonight, it didn't sound like it. Here's another wrinkle to your theory. I spoke to a couple of his employees out here. They knew all about Duncan and Ivy. According to them, Duncan was making plans to sell his business and move to California with Ivy. He even made her a beneficiary on his life insurance policy too. That doesn't sound like a man plotting murder."

"No, it doesn't. Perhaps he didn't plan to murder her but something happened that night to set him off."

"It's possible, but the guys I spoke to also said that Ivy sent Duncan a Dear John letter after she left. She told him that she never loved him and was just using him for his money. She then admitted to the thefts and told him not to look for her. They were really worried about Duncan after he received that letter. Said the letter was like a punch in the gut. Told me they started taking turns watching over him. It took years for him to recover."

"Ivy didn't send that letter. The letter had to have been sent by her murderer."

"I agree. I'm just not convinced Duncan was the one who killed her. I'm on my way home now. We'll talk as soon as I get back."

Leaning her hip against her desk, Arden said goodbye and then laid her phone on the desk. Soon she was pacing as she worked to put all the pieces of the puzzle together.

The murderer had to have known about the affair with Duncan. The Dear John letter proved it. So, who else knew that Duncan was planning on marrying Ivy?

Her brow furrowed in thought. Todd knew but why would he kill Ivy?

Jealousy?

She immediately dismissed that thought. He wasn't at Savannah's house the night Bruce died and he was too big. The killer had to have been someone small enough to wear Paige's boots.

Which means the killer had to be a woman.

Including herself there were six women remaining in the house when Bruce was poisoned. Out of those six, Paige and Savannah were with her when the killer borrowed Paige's boots. The only women remaining at the end of the party were Wendy, Emma and Julie.

So, which one knew about Ivy and Duncan's affair?

Wendy thought Ivy was having an affair with Todd not Duncan. If the murderer killed Ivy because of her affair with Duncan, then that let her off the hook. Of course, it's possible she could have been secretly in love with Duncan for years and wanted to get rid of the competition but . . . Wendy didn't sound very guilty from that snippet of conversation she and Max overheard tonight. Why would she be considering calling off the cremation and burying Bruce if she had poisoned him? Duncan seemed more concerned about it than she did, but that could be because he thought she was guilty and was trying to protect her.

Arden stepped out of the library and walked aimlessly down the hallway towards the kitchen as she tried to work out what the killer had been burying in Wendy's yard. She stopped in front of the door to the backyard and looked out as more questions sprang to mind.

What was the killer doing in Wendy's yard four months ago? What was she planting, if not Ivy's bones? How did Ivy's bracelet end up buried in Wendy's vegetable garden?

A thought suddenly occurred to her. Maybe the killer was planting evidence. Maybe she wanted Julie or someone to find that bracelet.

The killer was safe as long as no one suspected Ivy was dead, but now that the truth was coming out, she was getting desperate. She'd naturally want to pin the crime on someone and Wendy was a perfect fall guy.

Clover meowing distracted her for a moment and she looked around for her kitten. It wasn't long before thoughts of Ivy and her murder recaptured her attention.

Everyone knew Wendy hated Ivy. All the killer had to do was plant a charm bracelet in the yard or a necklace in the house and then Wendy would become the most likely suspect.

That still didn't explain why Ivy was murdered, but she could at least rule Wendy out as a suspect now. It had to be someone else but what was the motive? Why did Ivy have to die? Was it because she was a thief? Did it have something to do with Duncan?"

A flash of lightning lit up the backyard drawing Arden's attention to the crepe myrtle tree and the hornet's nest in front of the window.

Arden's breath caught in her throat suddenly. She lifted a hand to her face as the memory she had been trying to recall came back to her. She remembered Bruce standing next to her in Savannah's house. She remembered the look on his face. She remembered him leaning closer. She remembered him whispering in her ear . . .

Ivy kicked over a hornet's nest in more ways than one in this sleepy little town, and then poof, she was gone.

Another memory surfaced. A different one . . . and then, all of a sudden, she knew who killed Ivy and Bruce and who was trying to frame Wendy and why.

A shiver went down her spine as the windowpane reflected the killer's face over her shoulder.

Clover meowed again, louder, more incessantly this time from somewhere in the kitchen.

"I just made some tea," the killer said with a peppy, innocent sounding tone of voice. "Would you like some?"

Chapter 18

Julie held out a teacup. "It's an old family recipe."

Arden's skin turned clammy at the thought of drinking whatever was in the teacup Julie held out towards her. She plastered a smile to her face and hoped she didn't look as scared as she felt as she turned around and faced the young woman. "Thanks, Julie, but I'm not really thirsty right now."

Julie's eyes hardened. "Really?" She looked disappointed for a moment then brightened. "It's really good. Please, just try it. I know you'll like it."

Not wanting to tip the girl off, Arden reluctantly took the cup and then pretended to take a sip. "Mmm. I hope you'll give me the recipe."

Satisfied, Julie nodded before turning towards the kitchen counter. "Who were you talking to a few minutes ago?"

Arden looked at the girl in confusion as she set the teacup down on the counter. "Emma was just here . . . She'll be back soon. She was just getting some things out of her car. Have you seen Clover?"

Julie didn't answer, instead she said, "No, I wasn't talking about Emma. I heard you talking to someone in the library after Emma left."

"Oh." She glanced around the floor searching for Clover. "No one." Her gaze landed on the walkie-talkie on the counter a few inches away. If she could reach it, she might be able to get Savannah and Paige's attention. "Just some friends."

"Savannah?" Julie bent over and retrieved a windbreaker she had laid on the floor. "Or Paige?"

With Julie's attention distracted, Arden swiped the walkie-talkie off the counter and quickly slipped into the pocket of her jacket.

Julie's head whipped around suddenly. Her eyes narrowed suspiciously, as she circled around the living room furniture.

"I was just talking to some friends back home," Arden said.

Julie grinned. "I thought this was your home."

"It is." Arden shrugged lightly. "I guess I haven't mentally finished the move." She smiled. "Well, I better go upstairs and get changed."

Julie eyed the teacup before stepping in front of Arden. "Aren't you curious as to where Emma is?"

Arden glanced up at the ceiling. "She's spending the night so I guess she's probably upstairs putting away her things. I should probably go and help her."

"She's not upstairs," Julie said, all pretense of friendliness gone from her voice.

Arden couldn't keep the anger from her voice as her hand gripped the walkie-talkie. She pressed the button, praying Savannah and Paige would overhear them and come to her rescue. "Where is Emma? What have you done with her?"

Julie looked surprised. "Done with her? What do you mean?"

"If you've hurt her—"

"Hurt her?" Julie's brow furrowed as she crossed her arms and gave Arden a disappointed look. "Do you think I'd hurt anyone? Me? Sweet, innocent, little me?"

"You can drop the act now, Julie. I know what you've done."

Julie clucked her tongue in mock disapproval. "Why, if I didn't know better I'd think you were calling me a murderer, Arden. That's not very neighborly of you."

"Well, if the shoe fits, Cinderella." She glanced down at the jacket covering Julie's hands and backed up a step. "Where is Emma?"

Julie's eyes shifted towards the pantry. "She's a bit tied up at the moment. Don't worry; she has Clover to keep her company."

Arden closed her eyes, relieved that Emma was still alive. At least for the moment. If she didn't come up with a way out of this mess, neither one of them was going to be alive much longer. "What are you planning to do, Julie?"

"Depends."

"On what?"

"On how much of that tea you drank." Julie stepped around the island, glanced down at the cup and sighed. She slipped her hand into her jacket and pulled out a gun. "Looks like we're going to have to do this the hard way." She shook her head. "The moment I heard Emma yammering on about those stupid hornets stinging Ivy, I knew you'd eventually remember what I said the other day about seeing the welts on Ivy's face." She chuckled. "I had no idea Ivy got stung that afternoon. When I saw her face, I just assumed someone had hit her at the party the night before. She had horrible taste in friends." She sighed regretfully. "I didn't expect you to figure it out so soon though."

"Yeah, well you shouldn't have said anything about her face, especially since you were supposedly on your way to college when she got stung."

"No supposedly about it. I was on my way. I got half way to school when I realized I had to kill Ivy. I snuck in here a little after five and hit her on the back of the head with Gladys Oakley's ugly looking vase."

"Then buried her in the backyard."

Julie nodded. "Right by the oleander bush."

"Is she still there?"

Julie pursed her lips together in an angry line. "I moved her bones to Wendy's garden when I heard you bought this place. I couldn't leave her here. Not with new owners coming in and fixing up the place. You might have found her."

"You're lying. She's not in Wendy's garden. I just came from there."

"You and Paige didn't dig deep enough," Julie said, frustration coloring her voice. "I told you exactly where I found her bracelet. All you had to do was dig a little deeper and you would have found her." She sighed wistfully. "And if you had, we'd all be watching the cops drive Wendy away right about now."

"What did Wendy ever do to you? Besides, being the object of your uncle's affection. Are you that jealous of her?"

"It has nothing to do with jealousy," Julie snapped. "Uncle Duncan happens to be a very wealthy man with a thriving business. You don't think I'm going to let him marry Wendy Grayson of all people, do you? Can you imagine living with her? What a nightmare. No, see, I've got a pretty good thing going here. Uncle Duncan takes very good care of me. He's a bit annoying at times," she confessed, "but I have everything I could ask for and I'm not going to let Wendy ruin that. I'm not going to let anyone ruin that."

Arden couldn't believe anyone could be so selfish or callous. To kill two people and then frame another for their murder was just heartless. "Is that why you killed Ivy? Because you didn't want to share your uncle with her?"

"No, I killed her because she caught me stealing from the Oakley's and threatened to tell my uncle what I had done. I couldn't let that happen. If he found out I was the one behind all the thefts, he would've kicked me out. I had to kill her."

"You were the thief?"

"I needed the money. An allowance only goes so far. It's not like I was robbing them blind. A necklace here. A ring there. They barely noticed it."

"Gladys Oakley noticed."

She smiled. "Well, I had to make it look like Ivy left in a blaze of glory. I didn't want anyone wondering why she left so I made it seem like she had no choice. She's not going to show up with a warrant out for her arrest, is she?" Using the gun, she motioned Arden towards the French doors.

Arden held her ground, refusing to move. "You're making a mistake, Julie."

Julie narrowed her eyes. "I've made no mistake. I've been very careful."

"No, you haven't. You've been sloppy. Bruce saw you digging in my yard. He saw you coming in here at night."

"Yeah, so what? Now he's dead. Who's he going to tell?"

"And now you're making another mistake."

Julie paused. "How?"

"You went to all that trouble to conceal Ivy's body, even going as far as to kill an old man to keep her location a secret, and now you're purposely leading people to her. Isn't that kind of risky? What if the police find some evidence that implicates you? What are you going to do then?"

Julie smiled. "It'll never happen. I was very careful when I dug Ivy up and reburied her in Wendy's yard. I even dressed in Wendy's clothes and left a few of her hairs around, just in case. When they find what's left of Ivy, all the evidence I left behind will point straight to Wendy."

"It's still risky."

"Yeah, well, I'm not old like you and your friends. I'm young. We're risk takers." She looked perplexed for a minute. "I don't know why you all thought you could play detective. Shouldn't you all be rocking in your chairs on the porch or something?"

"We're in our forties, not our eighties."

"Yeah, well, I've got good news for you. You won't be getting any older after tonight. Now move."

Desperate to stall the young woman, Arden raised her hands. "But why frame Wendy? If you hate her that much, why don't you kill her like you killed her grandfather or Ivy?"

"Don't be stupid. She's not standing at death's door like that old man was and I can't just make her disappear like Ivy. I have to find a way to separate her from my uncle without drawing attention to me and I figure a long prison sentence will do the trick just fine." She looked smug for a moment. "It'll actually kill two birds with one stone. I get rid of her and ensure that no one will ever suspect me of murder."

"Is that why you placed Gladys Oakley's necklace in Bruce's room? Were you hoping Wendy would find it and wear it?"

"And she did too," Julie crowed. "I saw her wearing it this morning. Gladys Oakley must have worn that butterfly necklace a dozen times and Wendy never once noticed her or it. Was she wearing it when you all had lunch with her today?" Julie laughed. "I bet she was. I was watching you all from my bedroom this morning. What made you three run out of there like you did?"

"Wendy figured out that we suspected her of murder and was playing with us."

Julie laughed harder. "I filled her in this morning on what you all were doing. I knew she'd do something stupid and make herself look even guiltier. I made her swear not to tell you all that I was the one who told her what you were doing. By the time I'm done, there's not going to be a jury in the world that will think Wendy's innocent."

Thunder rumbled across the sky causing the lights to flicker for a moment. Arden prayed they'd go out long enough for her to get away but they stayed on.

Julie looked out the window in disgust. "What a miserable night. Well, at least no one will be out snooping around." A smile suddenly lit up her face. "And whatever evidence is left will be washed away. Perfect." Using the gun, she motioned for Arden towards the backdoor. "Go outside."

"Why? What are you going to do with me?"

"Isn't it obvious? You're going to have a little accident." She held open the door. "Those brick walkways out there can be so slippery."

"If you think I'm going to jump you're crazy."

Julie pointed the gun at Arden's head. "You can either jump or get shot. I'd much rather have your death look like an accident—less work for me that way—but I'm prepared to shoot you if I have to."

"You'll get caught."

"Wendy will get caught." Julie's fingers tightened on the gun. "This is her gun. I snuck into her house and stole it while you and Paige were in the vegetable garden tonight." She grabbed Arden's arm and pulled her towards the door.

Arden grimaced as the rain lashed at her face. "What are you going to do about Emma? It'll look suspicious if both of us have an accident."

"That's why poor Emma is going to commit suicide. The poor woman was despondent after having been fired by Wendy." She clucked her tongue. "Wendy is so cruel sometimes."

Arden pursed her lips together. "She's a nice woman. There's no reason to kill her."

Julie shoved Arden toward the back of the yard. "I don't know how many people you told about my little faux pas." She paused to wipe her wet hair out of her eyes. "If she goes around telling them that stupid hornet story they might figure out I was lying just like you did. Besides, you invited her to stay. You might say her death is your fault too."

A light went on in Bruce's room catching their attention.

Julie shoved the gun into the small of Arden's back. "Not a sound or I'll kill you right now."

They waited breathlessly for a few seconds until the room went dark. She heard Julie blow out her breath in relief. "Come on. Let's get this over with."

Arden's heart started beating faster as they neared the walkway. She held the walkie-talkie in a death grip, praying that Savannah or Paige had overheard their conversation and had summoned help. For a second, she thought she heard a police siren in the distance and her hope soared. Stepping out onto the walkway, she glanced towards the ocean. "No one is going to think I climbed over the wall and accidentally fell to my death."

"Sure they will." Julie reached into her jacket and pulled out a diamond pendant necklace. "This used to belong to Ivy. You see, I'm going to plant it on the other side of the wall just in front of Wendy's gate. They'll think you climbed over to retrieve it and fell." She clucked her tongue. "Such a tragedy but that's what you get for being nosy."

Arden glanced over the wall and down towards the beach. The closer they came to Wendy's gate, the sicker she felt.

Instead of thinking about it, she focused her attention on that siren and sent up another prayer to God as it grew louder.

Julie must have heard the siren too. She grabbed Arden's collar and began pushing her forward, hurrying her along the walkway.

Arden wanted to slow down long enough for the police to rescue her, but Julie was in a hurry now. She wasn't going to be able to stall the girl. With a sinking heart, she knew she was going to have to fight back.

Reluctantly, she loosened the grip she had on the walkie-talkie and slowly brought her hands out of her pockets. Her fingers curled into fists and she ducked her head, mentally preparing herself.

As she did, her gaze fell to the ground and out of the corner of her eye, she noticed through a bare spot in Wendy's hedge a pair of boots. Familiar looking boots with small pink beret wearing cartoon ducks on them. She blinked through the rain streaming over her face and focused on the ducks as the boots kept pace with them before disappearing from view.

A smile crossed her face as she quickened her steps, now in a hurry to reach that gate, knowing help was on the other side of the hedge.

Julie who was falling behind hurried to keep up. "Hey, what's your hurry?" She paused frowning at the open gate uncertainly. "What's this doing open?"

Just then, Savannah called Julie's name from somewhere behind them causing Julie to spin around in surprise.

Arden started to do the same when Paige appeared at the entrance to the gate. She grabbed Arden's arms jerking her back behind the hedge.

As they fell to the ground, Arden heard a loud thud followed by a groan of pain.

She crawled to the gate and peeked around the hedge.

Savannah, smiling ear to ear, stood over an unconscious Julie. "That's for calling us old."

Epilogue

Clover weaved her way through Emma's legs, meowing softly. "Just a second, sweetie," she said as she put the finishing touches on the cake she had baked. She stepped back and admired her creation a moment before picking up the cake stand it was on and carrying it over to the kitchen table.

Arden, Savannah and Emma all oohed and ahhed over the presentation before holding out their plates.

It was a celebration of sorts for the four. After one very long and dangerous week, they could now sit back and relax.

The killer had been caught and thankfully, everyone was safe and sound.

Emma despite being tied up and locked away in the pantry was happily getting settled in her new home. She had more than enough work to keep her busy between Arden, Savannah and Paige and she was tickled pink.

Paige had finally sold the pink cottage she had been trying to sell for months.

Savannah was relishing in being right and making sure her daughter-in-law knew it.

Arden was just happy to finally settle down and relax with her new friends.

Savannah glanced toward the partially finished backyard. "What are you going to do about your backyard now?"

"What I intended to do from the beginning," Arden said helping herself to a large slice of chocolate cake.

"I'm going to fix it up myself." She reached over and plucked a scrap piece of paper off the counter containing a rudimentary drawing of her backyard. "I drew this last night."

"That seems like a lot of work," Paige remarked.

Emma smiled brightly. "I'm going to help. I used to help my husband when we had a landscaping business. I know all there is to know about flowers and gardens. I think it'll be a lot of fun."

"And we've got all the time in the world to finish it," Arden added.

They glanced toward the front door as the doorbell rang. Excusing herself, Arden walked to the door.

Max stood on the doorstep with a brightly colored gift bag in his hands and Lucky at his feet. "Good morning, Sherbet."

Arden grinned noting with surprise that the nickname was starting to grow on her. Or perhaps it was just the way Max said it that she liked. "Good morning, Max." She bent down to greet Lucky as well. "And good morning to you too."

Lucky's ears lifted as he turned his attention from her to the kitten running towards them.

Max shortened his leash and held on as the enthusiastic puppy tried his best to greet Clover. Clover seemed less interested and contented herself by weaving around Arden's ankles.

"Lucky, sit," Max ordered.

Lucky laid down and rolled over.

Max shook his head with a sigh. "Oh well," he said holding up the gift bag. "This is for you."

Her cheeks flushed in pleasure as she took the bag. "You didn't have to do that," she said surprised by the weight of the bag. "Thank you."

"Well, I realized this morning that I hadn't properly welcomed you to the neighborhood, so I thought I better correct that."

Scooping Clover up, she held out the door. "Would you like to come inside? Emma's been baking . . ."

He smiled. "Lucky has an appointment with his obedience trainer today."

"Well, I definitely wouldn't want to keep you from that," she said watching in amusement as Lucky wrapped his leash around Max's ankles.

"I could stop by later," Max said. "That is if you're not solving any more mysteries in town."

She laughed. "I don't think you have to worry about that. My mystery days are behind me."

He inclined his head to the side, glancing behind her towards the back of the house. "Somehow, I don't think they are." He turned his attention back to her. "Well, I hope you like your present. Come on, Lucky," he said disentangling himself from the leash.

She watched as he walked away, wishing he could have stayed longer. As soon as he was out of sight, she turned her attention to the gift bag.

Smiling, she untied the pastel striped ribbon and looked inside the bag. Her smile quickly turned into a big grin as she peeled back the tissue paper to reveal a framed article from the front page of the local paper.

Local Trio Nab Killer!

Underneath the headline was a picture of Arden, Savannah, and Paige standing in front of Wendy's house and underneath that was an article about their efforts to solve Bruce McCallum's murder.

Clutching the picture to her chest, Arden opened her door and looked down her street as a feeling of pride swept over her.

She was finally home.

The End.

More Books!

I have three more books in this series written and will be releasing them one at a time over the next few months. You'll eventually be able to find them here at www.amazon.com/author/annabelallen.

Thank You!

Thank you for reading my book. I really hope you enjoyed it and if you did enjoy it, please consider leaving a review at www.amazon.com/author/annabelallen and letting me know that you did. I would greatly appreciate it and it will help me know whether to write more books in this series.

Sincerely,

Annabel Allen

Manufactured by Amazon.ca
Bolton, ON

12871444R00120